# Other Books by Larry M. Greer

*American Neanderthal*

*Appalachian Trail After Dark*

*Does God Play Golf?*

*The Ghost of Keowee*

*Heaven is in Union County*

*Soft Target*

# Tomb Society

Copyright© 2017 by Larry Greer

Printed in the United States of America

All rights reserved. Except as permitted under U.S. Copyright Act of 1976, no part of this publication may be reproduced, distributed or transmitted in any form or by any means, or stored in a database or retrieval system, without the prior written permission of the publisher or author.

This is a work of fiction. Names, characters, places and incidents either are the product of the author's imagination or are used fictitiously. Any resemblance to actual persons living or dead, events, or locales is entirely coincidental.

ISBN-13:
978-1544663548

ISBN-10:
1544663544

Cover Design by Rick Schroeppel
Elm Street Design Studio

# Dedication

An acclaimed 19th century author, Sir Pelham Grenville Wodehouse is credited with the observation that, "To find a man's true character, play golf with him." I am fortunate to have made fast friends with four such "characters". Through the course of a game of golf, they reveal both their strengths and weaknesses and provide me with 18 holes of laughter. Enjoying a round of golf with these men is one of my favorite pastimes. That is why I chose to dedicate this book to them and include them in this story: Geoff Golz, Ron Yatsko, Art Rodgers, and Peter Stanton.

Larry Greer
Tomb Society

# Acknowledgements

No book is better than its editor. It is virtually impossible for an author to create an impelling story; and then step back far enough to effectively edit his/her own work. We are too close to the tale we have woven. I consider myself very fortunate to have someone like Carol Browning who spent many painstaking hours, to not only check the mechanics of a book, but also ensure that the story line was consistent and accurate.

It is also critical for an author to understand if his/her book resonates with readers. Geoff and Linda Golz were both gracious enough to take the time to read through the manuscript and give me their thoughts. Thanks to you both for your support of this project.

# Tomb Society

**Larry M. Greer**

## The Heart Attack

The rhythmic beep of the heart monitor reached a fever pitch as a straight line shot across the screen and the steady beeping became the continuous note, foretelling death. As it always did in an operating room, this tone panicked the entire medical team. The two surgeons sprang into action. Dr. James Vance, the lead surgeon, barked at young Dr. Bob Robbins.

"Quick, get the paddles!" According to procedure, everyone else in the operating room stepped back when Robbins took the defibrillator paddles and placed them in position on the patient's chest. He pulled the trigger, resulting in a thud. Within one one-thousandth of a second, 3000 volts hit the man on the table. His body shot upward in response and then just as quickly fell back. All eyes flew to the screen as it changed to a small blip, indicating revival of a very weak heartbeat. As everyone held their breath, the man's weak heart, gave up its struggle once again and the monitor straight-lined for a second time. Robbins was ready with the trigger, but the end results were the same.

"One more time Bob, one more time." On the third jolt of electricity, there was no response. In his 68 years, Dr. Vance had seen his share of heart failure. He knew they had done everything possible to save this patient. Even with that knowledge, there was extreme sadness in his heart. Every time he lost a patient, he could feel bile moving from the knot in his stomach up his throat. What came next was what he loathed about being a surgeon...delivering the dreaded news to the patient's loved ones.

Vance swallowed hard and prepared to enter the room where the family was waiting. As he pushed the door open, he was staring into the hopeful eyes of four men nearly the same age as his patient.

"I am James Vance. Are you Mr. McNeill's family?"

One of the four stepped forward, "My name is Geoff and this is Ron, Art and Peter. We are not Jason's family, but his closest friends. We were with him on the golf course when he had his attack. Jason is not married and his daughter lives in California. Is Jason going to be o.k.?"

"Gentlemen, I am deeply sorry, but your friend Jason, did not make it through surgery. We did our very best, but his heart was just not strong enough to withstand the attack."

There were tears in Ron's eyes as he absorbed the painful news. The five of them had become like family over the past ten years.

Dr. Vance continued. "Given that there is no family present, I will have to rely on one of you to get in touch with his daughter. I know this is difficult, but we need to know her wishes about Mr. McNeill's body." Now, it was now Art's turn to choke up. To hear his dear friend referred to as merely 'a body' was more than he could bear. He turned toward the window to hide the tears welling in his eyes.

"I have already contacted her. She knows about his heart attack," Geoff responded.

"In that case, please stop by the emergency room on your way out and give them his daughter's phone number. The hospital will take it from there."

Vance noticed the utter despair on the four men's faces. He turned to go, but paused. "I am so very sorry that your friend, Jason, is not leaving here with you. I hope he had a good last round of golf."

"Peter spoke up and said, "Jason was one of the best golfers I have ever played with. Up until..." for a few moments Peter could not complete that sentence. "...his attack, he was beating all of us."

"If you fellows need to stay a while, please feel free to remain in this room to make your calls. If you would like me to speak with Mr. McNeill's daughter when she arrives, get my office number from the emergency room attendant." With that, Dr. Vance shook each of their hands and closed the door behind him.

Geoff sunk into the chair and took a deep breath. Each man was attempting to deal with the loss of their friend in their own way. Finally, not knowing what else to do, Geoff pulled his cell phone out and for the second time that afternoon, called Jason's daughter, whom he had never met. On the third ring Mary answered. From Geoff's call several hours before, Mary knew her father was in the hospital. When she saw Geoff's number on her phone, she didn't bother with formalities. "How is my dad?" she asked anxiously.

Geoff took a deep breath and paused as he looked around at the others for support.

"Mary," Geoff said in a quiet voice, "Mary, I am so very sorry, but your dad did not make it through surgery."

"Oh my God, my daddy is gone?" Geoff could hear the grief in Mary's voice.

"Mary, my friends and I are here to help you in any way you we can. You may need to think about it, but the hospital will need to know where you want them to send him."

"Oh Geoff," Mary sobbed, "This is almost more than I can handle right now. I know you are dad's friends and I hope I can lean on you for a while. I am not very familiar with Greenville and don't know what I should tell the hospital. Could you advise me? I've made flight arrangements that will bring me into Greenville tomorrow morning, but I need to at least be able to tell the hospital where to send him."

"Mary, your dad and I have been to a couple of funerals together at Mackey Mortuary. I think he would be comfortable with you sending him there."

"That sounds fine with me, Geoff. I will let the hospital know when they call me. I assume you gave them my phone number?"

"Yes, Mary, I'll do that." Geoff let Mary know that he would pick her up at the airport and give her keys to her dad's townhouse. Mary thanked Geoff and hung up.

****

Weather permitting, the same 16 guys played golf together every Friday. This had been their habit for more than 10 years. New members were invited into the small group as others gave up the game or moved away. It was on such a Friday that Jason McNeill had his heart attack.

It was a typically muggy August afternoon. The weatherman predicted a high of 94 degrees by two o'clock. There was not even the hint of a breeze to cool the four golfers as they waited patiently for the ladies in the foursome ahead to search for a golf ball in the rough. To stave off the sweltering heat, Peter had iced down 6 cans of beer in the back of his cart. Now six beers might seem a bit extreme for an afternoon of golf, but not for Peter. No matter the quantity, he never seemed phased. The other three were addressing the heat with wet towels wrapped around their necks. Geoff took a glance at Art, who was hoarding the only shade near the tee box. Geoff was alarmed at the beet-red color of Art's face and suggested to Art that he pilfer one of Peter's beers, even if was only to place the cold beer on his neck. When the women were finally out of range, Peter let one fly straight down the fairway and raced over to the cart to open one of his cold beverages and hand another one to Art. He told Jason, "It was really dumb to play in this heat."

"Ya!" Jason mumbled. "If we play next week, we have to get a really early tee time, or you can forget me. To be honest, I'm not sure I want to finish the round. When we make the turn at hole #9, I might just head home and turn up the air."

"Can't say I blame you," Peter agreed." If I had any sense I would quit as well, but these beers will keep me cooled down."

On the par-three 8th hole, Jason held back until Art, Geoff and Peter had hit their ball before he got off his cart and with great effort pulled a five iron out of his bag. Last December he had had a hole in one on this par three. "Not today," he thought. Merely the walk from his cart to the hole was a major effort. His vision was out of focus and his balance was a little wobbly. "Boy this heat is *really* getting to me," he thought. He had just celebrated his 79th birthday and although he was in reasonably good shape for his age, today he found it hard to walk without a shuffle in his step and each breath came with effort.

As Jason approached the tee, he thought, "Something is going on in my body and it not's good! I've never felt a pain like this in my neck and my shoulder's hurting like hell." Still, he said nothing, as he had never been one to complain.

Jason's friends watched him bend over to put his tee in the ground. Half way into that movement he just stopped. It was obvious that he was using his club for support. As Peter took a big swig of his beer, he realized that something was wrong. He jumped off their cart and rushed towards Jason. But before Peter could reach him, Jason's knees buckled and like slow motion, the club fell away and he dropped to the ground.

Peter wheeled towards Geoff and Art shouting, "We have a problem here. Jason seems to have passed out."

Geoff, a former military and private pilot, was trained to handle medical emergencies, He shouted back to Peter, "I am calling 911! It looks like a heart attack. Get something and raise his head, and Art, put a wet towel on his forehead to cool him down." The call was made and an ambulance from Salem, about 8 miles away, rushed, sirens blaring, toward the golf course. The fire department was less than a mile away and sirens, of these first responders, could also be heard as they sped toward the course from the opposite direction. Firemen were on the fairway within 7 minutes from the time they received the call, rushing a defibulator and an oxygen tank toward Jason. In anticipation of this, Geoff had already cut Jason's golf shirt open.

A mighty shock was released into Jason's chest and his back lifted inches off the ground. As everyone stepped back to give the firemen room, they shot another shock of electricity into Jason. This one caused him to groan. There was an audible sigh of relief, realizing that Jason was still alive. The fireman took his pulse. "His heart is beating, but the pulse is very weak." Moments later the EMS truck screeched in behind the fire truck and the medics appeared with a stretcher and more oxygen. Jason was placed on the stretcher and into the ambulance. Geoff jumped in beside Jason and told the others to join him at the hospital. He and Jason had been buddies for over 12 years and they saw each other several times a week both on the golf course and in the club.

As the ambulance raced south on highway 130 towards Seneca, with siren blaring, there were tears in Geoff's eyes. Jason was not moving, his eyes were closed and he was probably being kept alive purely by the oxygen. The emergency room was alerted and attendants met the ambulance at the door. Jason was rushed through the Emergency Room and directly into an operating suite. Two cardiac surgeons and three assistants were waiting. The lead surgeon took one look at Jason and knew he would be opening Jason's chest for a bypass. This was an experienced team. The operating room nurses inserted an electric pump into the artery in Jason's groin. This would keep blood flowing to his brain so the repairs could be made to his heart.

Art, Geoff and Peter waited in the room that was set aside for family. Jason lived by himself and his few relatives were all on the West Coast. Geoff had taken Jason's cell phone and searched for his daughter's phone number. He was able to reach her, but found it difficult to share the alarming news about her father. She was helpless to do anything from California, but told Geoff that she would get a flight the next day and thanked him for calling. When Geoff came back into the waiting room, Ron had made it to the hospital and was as upset as the rest of them. Ron and Jason had been like brothers. They would sit at the Club's bar and agitate each other endlessly. Mostly the ribbing centered on the veracity of their golf score or current politics. Even though these two were polar opposite politically, they didn't let that come between them. The four friends watched the clock and waited for word of Jason's surgery. They talked about how long they had known him and the crazy times they'd had together. One of the favorite points of contention was their backgrounds. The four of them in the waiting room were from 'up North,' while Jason was a dyed-in-the-wool Southerner. They reminisced about Jason's reputation as an exceptional young golfer and how the local pros and many of his long-time friends had encouraged him to try qualifying school and see if he could make the cut. But at a young age, Jason moved to California where he had a good job. He met his wife and they had a beautiful little girl. So, he had responsibilities! Jason continued to play golf, but just could not bring himself to leave his job and do what it would take to become a professional golfer. Sadly, after years of marriage they had gotten a divorce and upon his retirement Jason decided to move back home to South Carolina. So at 79, he was living in a golf resort on a scenic mountain lake and enjoying life...at least until that Friday!

\*\*\*\*

My name is Jason McNeill and I want to tell you the rest of my story that fateful day. You might not believe it, but it is the truth! My story takes up the afternoon that I died on the operating table. Guess I should have taken better care of myself, but you know us Southerners. We love our salt pork, grits and gravy!

Everyone has heard tales about "out of body" experiences, but most *rational people* dismiss these stories as fantasy. Well I did too! I had read a book several years ago about a doctor who described his personal "out of body" experience. Now, he is making a very good living telling this "fantasy" to audiences around the country. The major difference between him and me is that he is still living and I am very dead. So, posthumously, I am publishing my story and not enjoying any of the profits! It was an incredible experience during my time in that limbo state (Catholics call it purgatory). That's where you wait, before heading to Heaven or that *"Other Place."* At this writing, I am still not sure which <u>*place*</u> I will be assigned.

There have been many reports about 'out of body' experiences during moments of near death, but then becoming conscious again, and seeing lights overhead. Not unlike these stories, I felt like someone else was on that cold steel table. I could feel, as much as see, what was going on below me on the operating table. My chest was being split open. There was a lot...and I mean a lot of blood. I could hear the surgeon's conversations throughout the operation and there were a few moments that I actually thought they would get the old ticker going again, but as you already know, I kicked the bucket! That great Southern fried chicken had clogged all of my major arteries. I sensed the same panic that Dr. Vance felt as I was going over the edge from life to death. I could see it on his face. Once he knew he couldn't drag me back to life, I watched as the surgeons neatly stitched up my chest. I was never going to enjoy a normal life, ever again. I could feel hot tears down my cheeks and had a weird impulse to vomit as I felt the tubes being dragged from my throat and nose. The oxygen mask was removed by the anesthesiologist and hung back on the machine ready for the next cardiac victim. In the past few hours I had become attached to that oxygen mask...literally. It kept me alive a little while longer. And this was the hardest part. They pulled a sheet over my body, and my face, and just left me lying there on that ice cold table in the operating room. Talk about abandoned! I felt a real sense of despair. What would happen next? When I thought it couldn't get worse, I saw two masked hospital attendants in sterile blue outfits, enter the room. This couldn't be good! They slid my body off that stainless steel table and plopped my flabby butt onto yet another cold slab. This one had wheels. Then they covered me with another sheet and pushed my body down the hall into a dimly lit room that held three other lifeless lumps under sheets. It was cold in this room and I intuitively knew that I was here until they could decide what mortician would arrive to take me away. I really hoped Geoff would remember that I liked Mackey Mortuary...well as much as any person can like a mortuary.

I really didn't want to hang around in this very depressing and cold temporary morgue. Amazingly, I still seemed to have the power to levitate. So not seeing anyone around, I 'levitated' down the hall and through some big doors. A few nurses were heading my direction. I was curious to know if I was visible, but when I looked into the glass across the hall, I could see myself standing there naked. Evidently I was not visible, as none of the nurses either screamed or whistled. That was the moment that I caught a glimpse of my friends in the family waiting room. The doctor was talking with them in a very low, calming voice. I wanted to shout and say, "Here I am, here I am!" but I had no voice. So I just hung around outside the door and picked up all the details of what had happened to me. Then, I listened to Geoff as he made the call to my daughter in California. At first, it was very confusing and I found it hard to accept that I was really, truly dead and would never come back to my old life. However, I had somehow become one of those spirits that some people believed in. So what was I supposed to do? The one thing I did know was that I did not like this spirit thing and wished that I could just go ahead and completely die. As wrinkled and out of shape as it was, I really missed my body. So, I decided to go back to the morgue. Weird...now I felt comfortable melding my spiritual being back into my dead human body.

There I would wait for the morticians to carry me to the funeral home and after that, I had no clue. Would I continue to have this spirit ability? I didn't know and I did not want to think about it right then.

Larry Greer
Tomb Society

\*\*\*\*

After what seemed like a very long time, I felt that my body was being placed into that infamous black bag by a couple of young guys dressed in black suits. They were very respectful of my body as they slipped the zipper from my toes up over my face. At first I felt claustrophobic and thought, "I won't be able to breathe!" Of course, I did not need any air. I am dead, right? As they were rolling my body towards the doors, it crossed my mind that those other three bodies, still laying in the temporary morgue, may have been spirits as well. I wished now that I'd had more time to attempt contact. I was now riding on a drop-down stretcher in an unmarked black panel van. I could feel the sensation of hitting pot holes and stopping at red lights. My curiosity got the best of me so I separated my spiritual being from my body and kneeled down to see out the two rear windows. I watched the scenery go by as they drove through town, and I thought, this just might be the last time I would ride down interstate 385 and highway 291. This route would take me to the Mackey Mortuary. Way too soon, the van stopped and backed up to the rear door of the mortuary. Although I might never see Greenville again, I knew I would take one more ride...in a hearse to Woodlawn cemetery. I don't have a clue why, but I dreaded what was coming next. I knew, or thought I knew, what morticians did to dead bodies, and for some reason I did not want to witness this. Being embalmed was the last indecency...taking away my body fluids. Well, I'd never take a piss off the back porch again and never have to blow my nose. What the hell, the surgeons had already cut me wide open, so how could this be worse?

So I separated my spirit once again and decided it would be 'educational' to see what really did happen in the embalming room. Of course, I expected the embalmers to be very respectful of their customers and in this case I was right. I noticed from the number of bodies in this room, they were going to have a busy couple of days. The two 'suits' that had picked me up at the hospital, zipped down my black bag and slid me out onto yet another cold table. So many tables! This one was different than the operating table. While this one was also stainless steel, it had wide troths on both sides, and it tilted down at the bottom. I was later to find out that was for drainage of all those fluids that I cherished. Soon, a woman in her 40's, dressed in a white medical jacket, came towards me. She wore a hairnet, a nose mask and protective glasses. With all that on, I couldn't tell if she was cute...like I should care? I did observe that she had earbuds stuck in her ears. Although I figured she was listening to music, I actually hoped it was Rush Limbaugh on the radio and in my spirit form I could hear him too...just one more time. I always loved to listen to Rush and knew I would miss him in the afternoons. None of my golfing buddies tuned him in because they just couldn't deal with the truth.

I was a little embarrassed when she walked over to me and stripped the sheet off my cold 'necked' body. Did she not have any respect for a dead helpless man's body? She reached under the table and pulled out a sheet that was of a rubbery material and placed over my privates, which looked damn small from my point of view. In my younger years, I had been told by a few ladies that I was a prize, but not today. So, her small rubber pad was evidently big enough. I am sure she had seen more dead ones than live ones. The next thing she did turned my stomach. I say that, wondering how I could possibly still feel emotions.

The part that made me cringe involved a stainless rod about one foot long. It turned out to be an oversized needle connected to a plastic tube. I waffled between curiosity and the need to turn my head away as she selected a spot just about one inch above my belly button and pushed until the skin broke. Then she continued pushing until it connected with my large intestine. Suddenly an electric pump made an ungodly sucking sound. Soon I could see dark stuff flowing through the tube into a larger glass container. There went all my stuffin's. When the "stuffin's" approached the top of the glass container, she turned on a valve and it began emptying down a drain. My guess is that part of me is now on its way to the disposal *plant below Greenville*. Once all the fluids were gone, I was white as snow and my body looked drawn and even more wrinkled. Damn, I really looked awful! I hardly recognize myself. I must have lost ten or twelve pounds in 30 minutes. Suddenly, I remembered that Ron always said that I was full of it. Well, I guess he was right.

Now she yanks the sheet off and pulls yet another gigantic needle from her implement table. This one is also connected to a rubber tube. She shoves the needle deep into me just above the navel and starts filling me with embalming fluid. Perhaps this would smooth out some of those wrinkles and make me look a little younger! You know embalming fluid just keeps your body from decaying until the funeral is over and makes sure you don't stink up the place...one last time. I hated to put you through this process, but it is what it is. Most people don't ever think about it, but flowers at funerals, in the old days, were there to camouflage the odor coming from their loved one. Now I had to endure one last indignity. She actually sewed my eye lids and my mouth shut. She must have known my sense of humor.

Now it begins to get a little better. I got a makeover! I can honestly say, this is the first time in my life I've worn make-up. It doesn't look half bad! She gave me some color, thank goodness. She shampooed and styled my hair. She parted it on the wrong side, but no one will notice? There was one thing she didn't do. She had not bothered to brush my teeth. Hell, they hadn't bothered to put my teeth back in my mouth. That was not good!

While I was busy at the funeral home, Geoff and Peter had gone to my townhouse and knowing where I hid my key, let themselves in. They went upstairs to my massive closet and found the outfit I had worn to my 60th high school reunion a few months back. I had jokingly told them at a cocktail party several weeks before my death that I wanted to be buried in this classy outfit. Those designer jeans and pink linen jacket had been a bit pricey, but what the heck, you only live once. Geoff and Peter had then driven to Greenville to drop off the clothes and pick up Mary and Anna, my granddaughter, at the airport.

Having completed my embalming and my make-over, they pushed into a holding room. It was there I would stay until my daughter Mary could arrive and pick out my casket and handle the financial aspects of my death. All this would have been tiring...if I'd been alive. So, I decided to just settle down in my well-dressed body (minus shoes of course) and wait for Mary's arrival.

## 6:00pm That Same Day

Geoff and Peter had made it to Greenville in plenty of time, so they decided to make a stop at Peter's favorite bar - Twin Peaks, to kill some time with a few ice-cold beers. If I told you Peter could drink a gallon of beer at one sitting, I would not be lying. When they finally left the watering hole and headed for the airport, I am sure Peter felt warm and flushed.

Geoff had never met Mary, so he looked at each passenger as they came down the escalator. But it was Mary who recognized Geoff and Peter from their golf hats. After getting the baggage they headed straight to the funeral home, Anna reluctantly trailing.

I had become bored waiting for Mary and had drifted up to the lobby. I was there sitting in one of the chairs when Mary and Anna came in with Peter and Geoff. I cannot tell you the level of sadness that came into my spirit when they were standing there before me in the viewing room speaking with the young lady who would facilitate the funeral. Mary was a strong woman who had just turned 58. Watching her emotions, I felt like crying myself, but how ridiculous does that sound?

Anna took a seat in the lobby and started fiddling on her iPad. Mary asked Geoff and Peter if they would help her with the arrangements. As strong as Mary was, I could see the stress of the situation on her face. I really felt for her. Both Geoff and Peter just stood behind her and agreed with her decisions. I had done this before with my mom, for my dad's funeral and knew exactly how Mary felt. It made me proud that she had picked out a beautiful casket made of oak.

She came back to Greenville the next day with Geoff to visit a mausoleum. I was not sure I wanted to be placed in a tomb, but I had not dictated my preference, so I no longer had any say in the matter.

I had been dressed and placed in my new casket. You know, they had really made me look good. One thing I noticed was that I looked thinner and it showed in my plasticized face. Ron had sent over my five-iron...the one I had been playing with the day I died, and they put it in the casket with me.

Before Mary could say anything about what I was wearing, Geoff was quick to tell her that the clothes were what her dad had said he wanted to be buried in. Mary told Geoff, "Well, he always was a sharp dresser. And he looks good even in his casket." This comment made me puff with pride.

During my viewing, the afternoon before the funeral, all my golfing buddies that showed up, discretely dropped a new golf ball into my casket. And somebody dropped in a pint of Grey Goose near my hand. I suspect it was Art. Later I counted thirty two golf balls.

I know this death stuff makes you squeamish, but the story about my funeral will soon be over. You know, unless you are Huck Finn, you only get one in your life, so let me tell the last part before moving on.

Monday the service was held at the mortuary and there were wall-to-wall friends. They did a beautiful job and several made really nice tributes or told funny stories. It was the stories I loved. They were mostly true and they were entertaining for the mourners. I have always felt that a funeral service should leave a final and pleasant memory of the deceased. Mary of course, had chosen my closest buddies to be the pall bearers, with another twelve to serve as honorary. Mary and Anna looked so sad there on the front row with Geoff, Art, Peter and Ron sitting at her side.

Oh, I almost forgot, I was so uncomfortable inside that closed casket that I sat on the bench with Mary and Anna. At last the service was over and I was loaded into the hearse.

Thus started my last car ride out to Woodlawn and the mausoleum. There was no rider with the hearse driver, so I chose to sit up front and ride shotgun. Mary and Anna, along with my buddies, rode in the family car. I knew this was my last ride, so I took a good long look at my hometown. As the hearse turned into the Woodlawn cemetery, I caught a glimpse of The Clock Drive-in. I asked the hearse driver to take a detour, but I guess he didn't hear me. Oh, the memories I had of that place. I had eaten my share of 'all the way' hot dogs with fries and that probably contributed to this untimely ride to Woodlawn. A large crowd had gathered at the front of the mausoleum and witnessed me being pulled out of the hearse and carried inside. There were chairs set up for family. After the minister said his last words over me, Mary stood up and made some touching comments. Then it was suddenly over.

After my friends and family left, the workmen came and slid my casket into the concrete hole in the wall. I noticed they were going to seal it with a bronze plate. So just before they finished their work, I moved my spirit back into my body and was there when the final screws were turned.

# One Year Later

After having been entombed, I seemed to have gone into a long peaceful sleep, which is how many people envision death. After what I am guessing was about a year, I awoke in my dark casket and felt a strong urge to escape this crypt and move around. My mind was a little fuzzy, but then memories of my last days while alive were beginning to come back to me.

It must have been late at night when I emerged and stood on the carpet in the mausoleum. I looked down at my feet and realized I was still barefoot. Why in the Hell don't the funeral home guys put a pair of shoes in the box with you? I guess they never expect you to need them. The mausoleum entry had twenty foot ceilings with chandeliers that were softly lit. I stood there and listened, for what, I don't have a clue. But I do know that the silence was deafening. Suddenly I heard a small tinkling noise and I noticed it was the wind making the two glass front doors move just enough to create a lilting metallic sound. It was pitch black outside. I peered through the glass doors and could see the light from a few street lamps piercing the fog.

Larry Greer
Tomb Society

I gotta' tell ya, a mausoleum is a damn ghostly place around three AM in the morning, even when you are a ghost. To ease my nerves, I decided to explore this depository for the dead. There must have been several hundred people stuffed in boxes in these walls. The atmosphere could be best described as moldy, mingled with a small scent of room deodorizer, to mask the stale smell. As I studied the various names, I realized that I recognized a few of them. I smiled when I saw Vince Perone's name. He had run one of the best restaurants in Greenville and I had spent many a pleasant evening sitting at his bar. As I aimlessly wandered through the halls, I became aware that I was hearing another kind of noise. I thought it sounded like voices and the clinking of crystal. These sounds were coming from the back hall of the mausoleum. I was almost afraid to move in that direction, but curiosity got the best of me and I decided to head down the hall.

The voices were becoming louder as I made a cautious turn around the corner that led to yet another hall. Now the voices were quite distinct and I recalled those types of sounds. As I rounded the last corner I was astounded. I saw perhaps 40 or 50 people having, what would appear to be, a cocktail party. Who on earth would be weird enough to have a cocktail party in a place like this. Then I stopped and took a good look at the people. They were all dressed in fine party clothes. Some of the women had on long floor length dresses and the men were in suits and ties. A few wore sport coats with open collars like mine. I studied their faces. Like me, they were taught and their skin looked waxy and artificial...and none were wearing shoes. All of a sudden I realized these were people just like me...dead. Some were very old and a few were in their early 30's or 40's. They were all in animated conversation. One guy must have had a failed brain surgery. His head was shaven and the dark line half way around his head looked like it had been stitched with wire. A young guy, around 19, was even worse. I would later learn that he had been racing a Dodge Charger in his Corvette at over a hundred miles an hour when he was run off the road. I'll bet both those guys had closed casket funerals.

When I was about twenty feet from the group, somebody in the crowd looked over and called me by name. Hey, they could actually see me!

"Hey Jason, where have you been?"

I recognized this guy as Jimmy but could not remember his last name. I moved towards him, realizing I still had that killer sense of humor, and I responded, "I've been dead for about a year, what about you?"

"Same here", Jimmy responded.

"You know, the last time I saw you, Jimmy, was at our 60th Greenville High Reunion."

"You got it Jason. And I remember you were wearing that same pink linen sports coat and those designer jeans. What did you do, tell someone you wanted to be buried in that outfit?"

"Well, as a matter of fact, I did! By the way, Jimmy, how long have YOU been here?" I asked.

"It's been about four months. After the reunion, I found out that I had colon cancer and it didn't take long to do me in."

At that moment, my old friend Vince spotted me talking with Jimmy and rushed over.

"Hey pro, glad you had class enough to pick our mausoleum. I moved in the first week they opened this hotel with no check out desk. Did you play much golf before going down?"

"Oh, Vince, it's so good to hear you call me "pro" again. I never made pro, but sure wish I'd given it a try." I chuckled and continued, "As a matter of fact, I died playing golf. And by the way, I had nothing to do with the selection of this joint. Looks like my daughter Mary has the good taste in this family." Looking back at Jimmy, I asked, "What in the Hell is going on here? I mean all these people standing around...having drinks. Where did you get the booze anyway? And how can we drink, being dead?"

"Oh, some of us drop in on the liquor store down the street late at night and pick up what we need. I'll bet the owner of that liquor store is going mad when he takes inventory and comes up short."

I looked at the bar they had set up and asked,

"So, where do you keep all that booze and set up when you are not partying?"

Jimmy laughed, "You see that crypt just behind the bar. It's empty, so we take a couple of screws out the bronze plate and keep everything stored right there."

Vince turned to me and asked, "You still drink vodka tonics, guy?"

"You have a good memory, Vince. That would be great."

A couple of minutes later Vince returned with the drink in a nice Waterford crystal glass and chuckled, "OK, bet you wonder where we got the glasses, too."

"Well, the thought did occur to me."

"You remember ol' Heyward?"

"Ya, sure I remember him. We went to school together."

"If you remember, he had this really high-end jewelry and crystal store. Over the past few years since we formed our little society here in the mausoleum, we have paid his store a visit several times and collected a good number of Waterford glasses."

I just shook my head and looked around. There must be a couple of hundred people in this mausoleum. "Jimmy," I asked, "I see there are about 40 people here for the party, where are all the others?"

Jimmy responded, "It seems that a lot of the people entombed here don't really care about socializing, so they just keep to themselves and rarely come out of their boxes to join our 'Tomb Society'. You'll see some of them from time to time walking around the mausoleum halls like zombies. Most of them don't even speak to you. They are in denial that they are dead and trying to figure how to get out," Jimmy chuckled.

"Tomb Society! Are you kidding me, Jimmy? Is that what you call yourselves?"

"Neat name, wouldn't you say?"

"Kind of weird if you ask me."

Vince asked, "Would you like to meet some of the folks?"

"Sure, why not? Looks like the best way to cut the boredom."

Vince and Jimmy led me into the crowd and I met some of the older generation's movers and shakers of Greenville. There was a mayor and several lawyers. Vince pointed out, "The lawyers come in handy to settle little disagreements."

Now I thought that was really funny. "What kind of disputes are you talking about?"

"Well a good example would be whose turn is it to get to go out at night. The rule is that only 4 of us can be out after dark on any given evening."

"O.K., who keeps up with that list?" I asked.

"Hold on a minute Jason," Vince said' "I believe we have a little dispute going over there right now between Jack and Barry. Let's slip on over and see what it's all about. I think I know, but let's listen in."

We moved through the very talkative and animated residents of the mausoleum. Once we were near Jack and Barry, I could see that they were indeed embroiled in a serious argument.

31

Barry was jabbing his finger into Jack's chest and screaming accusations.

"God damn it Jack. The next time I catch you crawling in Sandra's casket, I am going to do something serious to you. What in the Hell do you think you are doing? She never could give a rat's ass about you. She's my wife, so go find another woman to hit on."

"And just what do you think you can do to me?" Jack asked.

"I'll tell you what I am going to do. When I catch you asleep, I am going to take your only clothes and you won't be able to come out of your box you ugly ol' bastard."

"You see Jason," Vince whispered, "That's why it's nice to have a lawyer around to offer an opinion and help settle quarrels." Vince turned to someone else and asked, "You sure we don't want Wally to intervene?"

"Who the Hell is Wally?" I asked.

"Oh, you'll meet him soon enough. He's usually near the front door so he can keep up with who is in and who is out at night."

"Is that all he does?"

"Oh no, but you'll find out soon enough."

What I had just witnessed between Jack and Barry blew my mind. Imagine a dead man sneaking into a dead woman's casket, and for what purpose? I really didn't want to envision that scene.

I looked around and saw a few attractive women and wondered how they had met an early death. But I would wait till later for that conversation. I looked down at my vodka tonic and remembered my earlier question. How could formless spirits like us drink? I mean where does it go? I had not taken a piss in over a year. So I mentioned this to Vince again.

"Jason that is a question none of can answer in here. Our guess is that somehow it just evaporates. We never get hungry so we never eat, and that's probably a good thing." Vince continued and smiled when he said, "There's only one toilet in the tomb and it ain't for our use."

I was very curious about many things, but I had to ask one more thing while we were on the subject.

"Vince, you say you have been here for about five years. My question is, when you go out to get the booze, how does that work?"

"We have to go very late at night; otherwise someone might see bottles of booze floating in the air."

It was all so confusing. With nothing else to do in a place like this except the weekly cocktail parties, I just laid in my 'box'. That is what everyone calls it in here. Sometimes I would not come out into the hall for days at a time. I guess it was days. Time is difficult to calculate when you are dead.

One night, I got up and headed for the Thursday night cocktail party. I guessed we had it in the dead of night because no living people came into the mausoleum after midnight and it was pretty safe to open up the crypt and set up our party. Tonight as I was meeting new residents, I overheard a very interesting conversation.

Marci was an attractive blond around 32, who had been laid to rest in a stunning black floor length dress with a beautiful string of pearls. She was talking with two other ladies about her recent trip. *A trip?* Perhaps I had misunderstood her. I had no clue that anyone in here could ever leave; much less go on a trip. When I had a chance, I sidled up to Marci and asked, "Hey Marci, I really wasn't eves dropping, but did I understand correctly that you left here and went on a trip of some kind?"

"Oh yes, Jason, I finely got up the nerve to take my fantasy trip. It turned out to be quite the adventure."

"OK, now tell me what you mean by a fantasy trip."

"Sure. If you are interested for yourself, you'll need to talk to Wally about the details. He's the one that has to approve anyone leaving the mausoleum.

"So here is what I did. All my working life, I was in the rag business. That means clothing. Most of the time I was in sales and worked for several famous designers, but I'd always had a dream of becoming a designer myself. If I had not killed myself in that damn wreck, I might have gone to New York and given it a shot. So after getting Wally's approval, I went to New York, just 6 weeks ago, and found myself in the luxurious offices of Designs by Scarlet De'Lando. Wally instructed me how to conform myself into the body of Scarlet De'Lando. This allowed me to take control of her design process and guide her hands. In doing so, I could actually get the feel of what it was like to be a designer. Scarlet never knew it, but through her body, I was holding her drawing pencil as she made sketches. I heard her tell someone that she did not quite understand the designs she had just created. I was in control of her hand, and making designs that were totally different from the style she had become famous for. She told some friends over drinks that evening, that it was like another person in her brain. What she said was: 'When I planned to draw a cocktail dress, somehow it turned out to be a long slim skin-tight gown. And I'll be damned, when I showed it to some clients, they went crazy over my new design. It was like someone else had taken control of my creativity at the design table.' Marci continued, "Her friends laughed it off saying that maybe she should lay off the martinis.

"I was there in my spirit form, of course, and heard the conversation. I felt a little like a scoundrel, but I also felt proud. After only a few of weeks, I had fulfilled my dream of designing clothes in New York."

"Fascinating story, Marci. I can't fathom doing something like that. Are you allowed to go on an adventure more than once?"

"Well, yes. Some have done it several times, but I am not quite ready to do it again, for a while. Guess I am just not that adventurous."

"Hey, tell me something Marci. I have come out to the Thursday night socials for weeks now, but I can't say I've ever met this Wally guy you all talk about. Can you point him out in the crowd?"

"Oh no, no, no, Wally is almost never seen among this group. The only time you'll see him is after midnight near the front door. If you act like you are going to try and sneak out of the mausoleum, he will be right there in your face. And believe me you don't want to get on the wrong side of Wally. Just between you and me, he's a little creepy."

****

As I lay in my casket staring at the lid, I could not get Marci's fantasy trip off my mind. With so much time on my hands, I got bored easily, so I thought a lot about what I would do on such an outing. Eventually, I drifted off and it may have been four or five days later that I heard someone tapping on my bronze plate. I figured it had to be one of my spirit friends paying a visit, but when I rose out of my coffin, to my surprise it was Geoff, Peter, Art and Ronnie. They were on their way to Twin Peaks. These guys liked to tell everyone that the attraction were the hot wings and man size beers, but everyone with half a brain knew they went to drool at the waitresses' "twin peaks." These boys were so anxious for their Twin Peak visit that they arrived in Greenville hours before the bar opened. That is what brought them by to see me...well they couldn't actually see me. I guess "pay their respects," was a better phrase. Sure wish I could go with them. Mary had given Geoff a front door key to the mausoleum. So there they stood talking quietly, and making jokes about me, but I knew all this bravado covered the sadness they felt without me. I felt the same. Since I had been in these digs for over a year, I was really touched that they came. Art was always the thoughtful one. He had laid a single rose on the floor below my crypt. As I watched them lock the mausoleum gate and walk away, all I could think was, "It sure is a good thing I can't still shed tears."

I returned to my box, but was restless. Seeing the guys made me want to be alive again and this place was so not exciting. With the exception of a few grieving relatives paying respects, all was noiseless. The halls were dimly lit and any sound reverberated off the high ceilings. I could smell the aroma of dying flowers, laid on the floor in front of a newly dead resident.

The fantasy trip idea kept racing through my mind. That was it. Tonight I would make contact with "Wally the creep".

When I heard the sounds of Thursday night's cocktail gathering, I headed towards the front entrance where Marci had told me I could find this guy, I saw no one. I stood there right at the door and gazed out into the stormy night. Rain was pelting the roads and occasionally a bolt of lightning spider-webbed across the sky. I had always loved the rain and was engrossed by the scene in front of me. Small bouquets of cheap plastic flowers quilted the graveyard. For the first time I became aware that there were two or three other mausoleums in the large cemetery and I wondered if they also had "tomb societies."

My intent was never to break out, but as I pondered the scene outside, I laid my hands on the push bar. While I had the ability to move through walls, I still had the sensation of touching objects. Holding a cocktail glass was an example. So, when I unconsciously rested my hand on the door, it made a little clicking sound. It must have been this sound that brought me back to the present. Suddenly, I found myself staring at a character straight out of a Charles Dickens tale. He was dressed in an aged leather riding coat that hung nearly to the floor. It was tattered around the lapel and his pants were held up with a very wide leather belt connected by a massive piece of silver. The trousers looked like canvas and were partially tucked into his knee-high boots. Even in this dim light, his shirt looked dingy. It was linked at the front with a thin black tie. The contrast of the ridiculously high collar and the dingy tie gave him a bazar appearance. His chubby face sat atop the high collar and his full cheeks were framed by bushy pewter side burns. His mouth was hidden behind a waxed mustache of the same pewter color but looked like twisted barbwire ending in tiny circles. This ensemble was concluded by a very tall top hat. Although the brim of his hat shadowed his eyes, I could tell he was looking at me. Silence reigned for what seemed like hours before he spoke. Living in the South most of my life, country accents were common, but his had a ring I could not place.

"Sir, were you planning on going out tonight?

Taken by surprise, uncharacteristically, I stuttered in my response.

"Uh, well, I was just looking. Is that a, a problem?"

"Please let me introduce myself. My name is Wally and I am gatekeeper of this tomb."

"Excuse me, what do you mean the gatekeeper of the tomb?"

"You could say that I am responsible for all souls or spirits, in this tomb."

I am thinking, "Marci was right! This guy is really creepy. He has both the odor and look of a very, very old soul and one <u>not</u> from around these parts."

"Wally, what good is a gatekeeper in this place? We're all dead!" I'm realizing that Wally must somehow facilitate these fantasy trips Marci was telling about.

"Well, what that means is, no one leaves this tomb without MY permission."

"Why would anyone <u>not</u> be allowed to leave this tomb?"

"Mr. McNeill, the rules here say that if anyone leaves without my approval, they will never be allowed to return to their body inside their coffin. They become lost souls, wandering out among the very dead. These rules are for all mausoleums and have been in place for a very long time."

"I have been here for about a year and never knew you could actually go outside. I've heard stories about late night trips to the liquor store and a crazy tale about fantasy trips. Tell me Wally, how does this all work?"

"It is very simple Mr. McNeill. All you do is make a formal request, and if it is reasonable, I will grant you a pass. It may surprise you, but most of your companions in this mausoleum never choose to leave. Some, here from the beginning, have never come out of their crypts."

"O.K., I'm really curious about this fantasy thing I heard about from Marci recently."

"Well, I can give you a one night pass without any trouble. If you have a plausible request, you could have up to a three week fantasy pass. However, you must be back in the tomb by the designated date and time, or you will never be allowed to come back into your crypt. You will wander, lost among the dead."

"So what could I do on a fantasy trip? I'd really like to get a change of scenery."

Wally began to tell me about how this all worked. Suddenly, Wally was not nearly as creepy. He actually seemed genuinely friendly. He explained that if it was a fantasy I wanted to play out required traveling a distance, he could show me how to move through time and space. Now this sounded cool!

"It is not hard. Once I allow you to step outside the mausoleum's front doors, you will remain still and concentrate on the spot where you want to arrive. When you do this for the first time, it will be a strange sensation; like awakening from a dream. You may find yourself among live people. It will take adjustment. You may experience the sensation that you are alive again, standing there in your pink sports coat and jeans, without shoes." Wally smiled and continued, "But no worries. No one can see you. They may feel a slight breeze as you brush past them." Wally continued, "Let's say for example you wanted to be a jet fighter pilot...a very exciting experience. If you need the help of a living person to experience your fantasy, you would have to integrate your spirit into the living person's body. This would enable you to live out your fantasy. In the case of flying a jet fighter, you would become part of the living pilot.

Through the pilot you would feel like you were actually flying the plane."

This just keeps getting better, I thought. "O.K., go for it. Tell Wally what you'd like to do and let's see what happens."

I decided to plunge forward and tell Wally. "So, this is what I have been thinking. When I was a young man, I loved to play golf and was actually pretty good. My friends encouraged me to take up the game professionally and apply for qualifying school. But I never could get up the nerve. Over the years I really regretted that decision."

Jason took a deep breath before continuing his conversation with Wally. The very thought of what he was about to reveal to Wally was exhilarating.

Larry Greer
Tomb Society

# Jason's Fantasy

Wally sat down on a bench near the mausoleum's front doors and listened to Jason describe his life's fantasy. As Jason suspected, Wally had lived several hundred years ago and knew almost nothing about golf, so Jason patiently explained the game.

"So, now that I know about this game of golf Jason, what exactly is your fantasy?"

I found that I could not respond. I was remembering all the things I had accomplished in my lifetime and all the others that I never got to achieve. If I could have been a writer, I would love to have had the talent of James Michener. Or, if I had been in an aviator, what would it have been like to be an astronaut? Everyone has but a short time to make something of themselves, but few actually pursue their dreams before their time runs out.

I looked back at Wally, "I missed my chance years ago to become a professional golfer. Although encouraged by friends, I just did not have the faith in my ability. I made the excuse that I had a wife and a little girl to take care of and I didn't want to risk my family's security. Many times I regretted that decision. Now it is too late. Do you know that

I was playing golf when I had the heart attack that got me here?

"So you ask what fantasy I want to experience," Jason paused for a moment and then continued. "Like millions, I've watched The Masters tournament in Augusta each year. I even had tickets a couple of times. If I could play out one fantasy, it would be to go to Augusta in April and make myself a part of the event."

Wally replied, "As you know, I am from another time. I do not know this 'Masters' you are talking about, but I know you could make yourself feel as though you were playing in the event. When would you like to leave and how long do you need to be there?"

"The Masters starts in two weeks and I need to be there for at least one week to realize my fantasy."

"That should work, Jason. Let me know when you are ready and I will be here to help you on your way."

Larry Greer
Tomb Society

# The Masters

I told Wally I needed to arrive in Augusta on Monday prior to the practice rounds, so I could take full advantage of experiencing the entire tournament. I wanted to plant myself in the bleachers and observe every golfer on the practice tee.

Wally approved of my fantasy and in one week I would be headed to The Masters. How could a dead guy feel such excitement? That concept baffled me, but I felt like I was experiencing that same exhilaration. I worked at lying perfectly still in my casket and yet restful sleep escaped me. On the Thursday night before I was to leave for Augusta I decided to attend the weekly cocktail party. I wasn't sure if telling about fantasies *before* they happened was permissible, but I just couldn't contain myself and told everyone who would listen, what my plans were. A number of the guys in the mausoleum were what we called "old duffers." Some were amazed and others scoffed at my plans. What exactly was I going to do once I could move, unseen, among the greatest living golfers in the world?

I confessed that I really did not know what was possible, but be assured I would live this fantasy to the fullest and do what living people in the crowds could *not* do.

Each time I had been in the gallery at The Masters I had the urge to step over the ropes...now I could actually do that and no one could stop me. I would walk down the fairway beside the pros and caddies and experience the tournament as only the pros did. "What a crazy idea you have Jason" the others would say. I knew their scoffing only masked jealousy and regret that they hadn't thought of it first.

Sunday night, in anticipation of the journey, I stood at the doors of the mausoleum and tried to imagine what I was about to experience. The ink black night was fading into silver as a full moon made its ascension into the sky. Suddenly I felt the presence of others. Jim and Vince stood on either side of me as I waited for Wally to instruct me on the most exciting journey of my life...oh ya, guess it would be "my after-life." The three of us chatted quietly. They patted me on the back and wished me luck. It was then I noticed Wally standing quietly in the shadows.

"You ready Jason?" Wally asked.

"Oh, I am sooo ready!"

"Ok then, I want you to go through the doors and stand quietly outside. You will close your eyes and concentrate completely on the very spot where you wish be just before daylight. Your spirit will transcend exactly to your desired destination. You will feel strange sensations of floating in space. Your spirit will be suspended in time until the appropriate hour. At that point, you will find yourself at the Augusta National Golf Course. Do not forget, you *must* be back here at the tomb before midnight on the following Sunday. If you want, you can return before that appointed time, but no later than Sunday night at midnight. Whenever you return, it *must* be after dark."

"Just one more question Wally, do I have any options for a change of clothes? It may be warm down there."

"Jason, you will learn that what you were buried in is your permanent attire. You cannot change clothes and you cannot take off your coat Jason. Remember, as a spirit, you do not feel the discomfort of either heat or cold."

I took one last glance back at the mausoleum, turned and floated out through the glass doors. Once outside in the silver light of the moon, I stood perfectly still, as Wally had told me. Then after a few moments I closed my eyes. Up to this point, I had felt brave; but now, I sensed queasiness in my being. Just what was about to happen? I gritted my teeth and began to concentrate totally on the Augusta National Golf Club's front gate. I have no clue for what amount of time I stood in front of the mausoleum, but I suddenly had a sensation of being be jettisoned through space. My being slowly spun end over end, rolling and tumbling. Had I been alive, this would have made me vomit! I sensed, more than saw, brilliant moonbeams in the shadows and highlights of a rainbow. A star-clustered sky was shielded with a thin layer of silky clouds that extended into the heavens. Was this what the druggies experienced? If so, I understood why they were addicted. I experimented with moving my limbs. In a daring moment when I turned 40, I parachuted out of a perfectly good airplane. Never again, but this was that same feeling, only definitely scarier. I was being thrust horizontally at lighting speed through the stratosphere. I wondered how my $500 pink sports coat and $200 designer jeans would make this trip.

My concentration was to land just outside the main gate. If you can worry as a spirit, I was stressed about what the landing would be like. I decided to concentrate on a soft landing and see if that would work for me. It must have worked, because if a spirit can lose consciences, I believe I must have. For when I opened my eyes, I was hovering a foot above the asphalt, smack-dab in front of the main gate of the Augusta National Golf Club. Aaamazing! My first thought was to check my attire. Perfect! It was pre-dawn on Monday morning. The sun was announcing its appearance by gilding the leaves of the gigantic pine tree on Hole number 10. I was beyond elation! Even at this hour, early bird fans were beginning to gather, anxious to present their tickets, spin through the turnstiles and plant their chairs in just the right spot to see the winning putt on the 18th hole.

I wanted to have an experience this week that no living human could ever conceive. I did not know my powers or my limitations so I decided I'd experiment. I levitated among the early fans as they dashed past me toward an advantageous viewing spot on one of the gorgeous fairways.

As the sun sprayed brilliant hues of orange, gold and delicate rose across the canvas of sky, thin rays were peeking through tall Loblolly pines that stood like sentinels around the perimeter of the course. A light fog rose from the sunken areas of the creek that meandered through the famous Amen Corner. A sea of perfectly manicured emerald grass, blanketed by early morning dew, stood ready to be trampled by thousands of feet that day. Dazzling white, delicate pink and brilliant red azaleas, accented by yellow jonquils, outlined the fairways. As if this picturesque scene were not perfect enough, birds added their music, foretelling an unforgettable day for Jason McNeill. Humming lawn mowers could be heard in all directions ensuring the greens would be manicured to perfection. This was the most spectacular garden spot in the world, every year that first week in April. Millions would be watching as the best golfers from across the globe would compete 4 days for the crown jewel of golf and that coveted green jacket.

I decided to saunter out to the practice range to see what early bird was up hitting balls. Some of the pros edging toward the Champions category, preferred to practice early and get their 18 holes in by one o'clock. The really young bucks, after partying late the night before, would savor those extra hours of sleep. Fans were beginning to trickle into the stands behind the driving range. These die-hards would be around all day and stay to see the last golfer play the 18th hole at sunset.

*****

Practice putting greens were situated so spectators could get close to the pros. I decided to join them and see who was practicing. Wow! Tom Watson and Gary Player were two of the early birds, putting and chewing the fat. These two guys had always been among my favorites. In my mind, their combination of talent, class, and sportsmanship set the perfect example for up-and-coming young golfers. They were truly the 'gentlemen' of golf. Still not sure about the ability of my 'spirit' form, I had a mischievous thought. If I could hold a real cocktail glass back at the tomb, I could probably alter the movement of a golf ball on the green. So, I floated through the ropes and onto the green near where the pros were putting. My plan was to mess with a pros' mind as he made a rather simple short putt. So, I got down on my knees near the line of the putt. As the ball rolled past me, I gently tapped it with my finger and moved it slightly off its intended path. The pro doing the putting, was surprised at the apparent subtle undulation on the green's surface. As many times as he had made this putt in the past, he had never noticed the ball break that way before. The next putt he made, I let alone and the ball dropped straight into the hole. Just to reassure himself, he tried the putt a third time. Again, I barely touched the ball and it went off line, ringing the hole. That golfer was Bubba Watson. I really loved to watch him play and always pulled for him. Before I died, he had been one of my favorite golfers on the circuit. I think I liked him because he was a lefty had the ability to hit some of the longest balls I had ever seen. Rumor was that Bubba never had a golf lesson nor did he want one. After all, he had won The Masters, so who could second guess that decision. My spirit body tingled as I hovered only a few feet from him. I just could not resist messing with him. So after the mystery of the break in the green caused him to miss three of his six putts, Bubba moved his balls around to another angle and set up to make a 6-foot putt. With vast experience on this course, he knew the ball would break just a half ball out of the hole on the left side, so he made his first putt. It was

Bubba's habit to always make six putts to the practice hole from every angle. He made the putt. Just as he had calculated, the ball made a slight break and dropped in. Now it was my turn. On his next putt, I taped the ball with my finger as it was passing me, making the ball break back to the left of the hole, just the opposite of the first ball. I watched Bubba's face and he just shook his head in disbelief. I wasn't sure whether I could be heard if I laughed, but boy I wanted to laugh. On his next putt, I again made the ball do the opposite of what Bubba was expecting. He was dumbfounded and asked Tom Watson to come over and try this hand at this green. "Tom, it is the craziest thing. My ball is breaking in both directions. You try it." Tom took a look at the hole and putted from exactly the same spot. Tom's ball went straight as an arrow into the hole.

Tom chuckled, "I don't quite see what you are talking about Bubba. Mine went in fine. Why don't you putt another one and let me see if you are doing something weird." Tom had become a mentor of sorts for many of the young golfers. So Bubba rolled a ball into place, lined the putt up straight, just as Tom had and putted. I decided not to alter the course of the ball and in it went, straight as an arrow. Bubba looked at Tom with his boyish smile and said, "I just don't get it. I mean I putted the other ball from exactly the same place before and it broke to the left. I have about an hour before my practice round this morning so I am going over to the range and hit a few long ones. Maybe I can get this weird stuff out of my head."

It dawned on me that I could really change the outcome of the tournament, but that was not what I came to do. I had too much respect for The Masters to fulfill my fantasy that way. Since I loved to watch Bubba play, I decided to follow him on out to the practice tee and watch him drive. One year after attending The Masters, I looked up his average driving distance and was impressed to find that it was 315 yards. Even more amazing, when he hit it wide open, he could exceed 330 yards. Watching Bubba drive was a highlight of many fans. I watched him warm up with a wedge and then a 7 iron before selecting a three wood. I had watched him drive on TV and from a distance in the crowd of The Masters years earlier, but being this close and watching that swing, I was in awe of the results he got with that sweet left-handed drive. After hitting six balls with his three wood, his caddy, Ted Scott, handed him that famous pink driver. Instantly, I remembered Marci's story about experiencing her creativity by guiding the hands of a famous dress designer. I wanted to do the same thing with Bubba.

I'm not sure the exact distance he was hitting, but the balls were landing high on the barrier fence, so that must be at least 300 yards. Behind the barrier were some very tall dense trees creating a barricade between the club and a heavily traveled road. I wanted to experience the same feeling Marci had, so I moved up to Bubba's back, just before he positioned himself to swing and I merged my spirit into his body. Now, if you think this sounds weird, you should have felt what I did. The strangest sensation was actually seeing through his eyes. I was standing on his feet and my arms were inside his. I wanted to see how it felt to hit a ball using his body. He momentarily shook his head as if trying to rid himself of something, then conferred with Scott, his caddy. He griped his driver and moved into his back swing. I made no movements to help him on this swing. I just wanted to experience it. And experience I did! It was better than a carnival ride. I was being swung around without control.

It felt like my arms were being pulled out of my shoulder joints. After Bubba had hit his third drive, I began to get the feel of his swing pattern.

In the middle of being 'inside' Bubba's body, I recognized a man from Greenville. Joe White was president of a new golf ball company. He was approaching Scott, to see if Bubba would test his new OnCore balls. Scott had known Joe for years. "You know Joe, it's against the rules to do that, but what the Hell, I'll let him hit one practice drive. Will that satisfy you?" Joe was pleased and I decided to have some fun with them both. When Bubba drew back his club, I tensed up and pulled back with him. I used all my 'ghostly' strength, hoping to give him a faster swing rate than he had ever experienced. I figured that if his normal swing rate was 128mph, with my assistance, we could take it to 145mph.

It worked. Bubba, Joe and Scott stood in amazement witnessing an unprecedented drive. His previous balls had been hitting the tall net in front of the pine trees; this ball climbed up and over those pines and landed across the adjacent road. As they followed the flight of the ball, they cringed as they recognized that distinctive sound of a car windshield being cracked. Bubba glanced at Scott and said "Damn, I think that drive was worth paying for someone's windshield!"

Scott was dumbfounded. "I don't know what to say."

It dawned on Bubba that he wanted to see if he could repeat this drive. "Scott, what kind of ball was that?"

Guiltily, Scott replied, "It was a new ball that that Joe White gave me."

"Shit, give me another one of those balls. I want to see if I can do that twice."

"Bubba, before you do that, perhaps I'd better make a call and increase your insurance," Scott chided.

Bubba chuckled and set up for another drive using an OnCore ball. I helped him achieve the same results. Moments later, a security guard rushed onto the driving range and asked Bubba if it was him who had hit a ball onto Washington Avenue.

Bubba confessed that it probably was his ball. Scott gave him a business card and promised that Bubba would pay for any damage done to the car.

Joe could hardly contain his excitement. This new technology had resulted in a drive with unprecedented distance. Only problem was that Bubba had made that drive with the OnCore ball, illegally. Joe couldn't tell a soul without getting Bubba in trouble.

But Bubba was not as sure as Joe that it was all about the OnCore ball. Bubba thought, "It takes a lot of head speed to hit a ball that far and there was more energy in my swing than I have ever felt before. It felt like I had an extra force in my back and follow through. I don't really think it was just the OnCore ball I was hitting that made the difference. It was like I found an amazing inner force."

Scott was shaking his head, "Bubba that was some incredible drive. Think you could replicate that on #1 this morning?"

"I don't know," Bubba responded. Joe handed Scott a three ball sleeve to put in Bubba's bag. "You know Joe, Bubba is under contract with another company. He cannot be caught hitting another manufacture's ball." Joe just waved a hand in dismissal and headed toward the club house.

I am thinking, "This is the way I can fulfill my fantasy of playing in The Masters. No one knows I am here and I'm invisible, so I can have a lot of fun. Problem is how do I use this gift without influencing the outcome of the tournament?"

\*\*\*\*

It was around 10:30am and the course was packed with patrons, anxious to watch the first day of practice rounds. Now that I discovered what latitude I had as a spirit, I figured I'd stroll up to the club house and have a look-see. Spectators were never allowed in the sacred space of Augusta National Club House. It was probably one of the most recognizable structures in the country, at least for golf enthusiasts. The building itself was stately, but not pretentious. Today, it felt warm and welcoming. In reality, it was welcoming only for the members, or professional golfers at The Masters and those specially invited. Of course I was not invited (that's a joke). I floated over the ropes that separated the commoners from the elite and stood on the lawn where drinks and lunch were being served to members under green and white umbrellas. I saw Jack Nicklaus having a Bloody Mary. Several tables over, Jack's wife was engaged in a lively conversation with Gary Player and his wife. If I could only make a selfie with them, to show Vince and Jim. Several tables away, Arnold Palmer was surrounded by an army of fans eager' to rub elbows. I was awed. Right before my eyes, on this beautiful April morning, sat the 'big three' in all their glory.

Not surprisingly, I spotted Joe on the back side of the deck, with a mimosa in one hand and a golf ball in the other, talking earnestly with a few other men. He must have been giving a quite sales pitch. I noticed others on the deck with drinks in hand, as well. Their glasses had tiny green umbrellas and a large garlic stuffed olive speared at the end. Those drinks looked so tempting. I had enjoyed vodka tonics back at the tomb, but I would not dare chance drinking a with red tomato juice, in case you could see it moving through my spirit body...so I moved on.

Larry Greer
Tomb Society

I knew no one could see me, but I was still nervous as I entered the club house to see the interior for myself. I believe they purposely do not photograph the interior of the club. I was a little surprised at the diminutive size of the main room. It was like a vestibule. Despite its modest size, the furnishings were plush and tasteful. Oriental rugs protected old pine floors. A few members were milling around, sporting their green blazers and enjoying the benefits of their membership. I spotted our Governor and a couple of U.S. Senators in conversation on the veranda. From this vantage point you had a clear view of 3 separate fairways. I was enjoying my private tour of the club house and it appeared no one could see me, so I wandered until I found the locker rooms. This search took me outside and into the lower level of the adjoining building. Surprisingly the main locker room was not well appointed. Like the famous lunches of egg salad sandwiches on white bread, they were under-stated. However, I wandered into a second locker room. Here the furnishings were significantly more upscale. This must be what you moved up to when you actually won The Masters. I moved around the room where several pros were changing into their attire for the tournament. The signs on the lockers made up an impressive list of 'who's who' in the golf world. My ears perked when I heard Bubba's voice. He was talking to Jackson about his frustrating putts that morning and telling him about the two drives that cleared the nets and trees adjacent to Washington Street.

"Some golf salesman slipped Scott a couple of balls I had never seen before. He took all the credit for the extra distance, claiming it was this new ball. I mean, Jackson, I never in my life hit a ball like that before...almost like it was jet propelled, clearing fence and tree tops. The crack of a car windshield confirmed it landed in the middle of busy traffic on Washington."

Jackson shook his head in disbelief. "Bubba, I'm not sure I can buy that story! You got a clue the distance and the loft of that drive?"

"You know Jackson, to be honest, I don't really know, and you'll think I'm weird, but I swear, it felt like I had an inner strength pushing the ball with me."

"Man, I need a ball like that. What was the brand?"

"Jackson, I can't honestly remember. Must be a new brand, because I've never heard of it before."

I eavesdropped little longer and chuckled to myself. The doubt you could see on Jackson's face reminded me that Bubba was not popular among many of the other golfers. But he was still *my* hero. I just loved the way this man hugged his Mom after winning The Masters in 2012. I figured he was probably a good guy and sometimes didn't know how to react to his own success. A magazine story written in September of 2012, made him out as a very private person who abhorred the media. I respected that and decided to continue shadowing him this week. I may mess with him a little bit more, but I certainly would not impact his play one way or the other. I wanted him to win...fair and square.

I moved along the stairs to the second floor. This area is known as the Crow's Nest. It was built as a sleeping loft for up to five amateurs. The guys that occupied the Crow's Nest this year fit the stereotype of 20-somethings: unmade beds and rumpled clothes scattered on the floor. They can stay here and cut their expenses while playing The Masters. This was a great addition for amateurs who could not share in the purse. Hotel rooms in Augusta the first week in April were outrageous and local homes rented for thousands of dollars that week. Continuing my self-guided tour, I found a big dining area used for the player's banquet on Sunday night following the tournament. Man what I wouldn't give to crash that event, but I knew I had to be back at the mausoleum Sunday before midnight.

Having satisfied myself with my tour of the club house, I drifted down to the first hole. 'Tea Olive' was 445 yard long.

All the holes were named for trees at Augusta. There was a crowd hanging around the tee area watching a threesome who had chosen to play a practice round together. You could tell from the banter between them that they were good friends. As I watched them, I felt old. They were full of themselves in their color-coordinated outfits. They flipped a tee to determine the order. Billy Morrow drew the short straw and teed up first. Billy was tall with a Brillo pad of blond hair. He could have passed for a young John Daily. He ripped his drive into the pines about 290 yards to the left of the fairway. He spun around with a stupid grin on his face, "Boy I knocked the heck out of that one." If there had not been a crowd around, you might have heard more colorful language. Brandon White teed up second. He had been the star of the Citadel golf team and later turned pro. Brandon was the epitome of what us old guys call limber backs. He topped off at 6' 2" weighing no more than 170. When he brought his club around and back above his head, it looked like he was going to wrap the driver around himself before he made it to the forward part of his swing. But his ball went straight down the fairway and fell just left of center about 295 yards. This set him up for an eight or nine iron shot to the green. Typically he was a quiet guy, but you could see a smug little smile run across his face as he came back to the group. The third to hit was an amateur that could not have been more than eighteen. Listening to this group I found out that his name was Jamie Joseph from Greenville. Jamie was in great form around five feet seven inches and sported a mischievous smile and a swagger as he punched a tee into the ground. Small guys like Jamie can fool you when it comes to blasting a ball into orbit and in this case his drive did not disappoint. I could not tell how far he hit, but it brought a roar of approval from those standing down the fairway.

Now I got it. These kids were all long ball strikers and the testosterone was quite palpable as they vied to out-drive each other. Of course, that can get you into a lot of trouble. My granddaddy once told me that the woods were full of long ball hitters. Their competitive nature could prove to be fun to watch, so I decided to follow these three for a while and see if any of them had a chance to qualify. On hole #1, all three made par. Hole number 2 was the infamous Dogwood hole at 575 yards. This would be fun! Dogwood was the longest of the par 5's and it was every pro's challenge to reach it in two. Very few made it. The hole was designed with a down slope that curved to the left all the way to the bottom. If the golfer could get his ball to land on the left side of the fairway, there was a chance of reaching the large green on the second stroke. For a long hitter like Bubba Watson, if he hit it right, he wouldn't see his ball land. The fairway was wide and it instinctively brought out the raging bull in the rippers. They all wanted to knock the day lights out their ball. I looked across the crowd and there was Joe again. Not surprised to see him, as Brandon was his son. Guess what ball Brandon was playing with? Yup...an OnCore! Not a problem this time, as Brandon was not under contract with any of the big-name ball manufacturers. I did not know Joe well, but liked the persistence I observed as he worked to get his unknown golf ball into the bags of as many players or caddies as he could.

Bill was still up. He hit a good ball but it landed just a little too far right. Brandon teed up second again. I decided to see if I could help him create some excitement and moved from behind him into his body. Brandon, being tall, was not a really good fit for me, but I managed to get my hands on the club with him and when he made the turn from his waist back, I understood how soft taffy feels when it is pulled and twisted. Back we went with the big driver and then a downward 'swoosh'. We returned the club back to the ball and completed the follow-through as only a young man can execute. Brandon just stood there frozen in his finish  The ball continued to gain altitude and just kept climbing until at last it began its descent.

His caddie was the first to realize just how far this ball went, "Brandon, I believe you just hit that ball close to 315 yards."

"I have never hit a ball that far. How in the Hell did that happen?"

Jamie and Billy immediately wanted to know what ball he was using.

Proudly Brandon admitted, "It's my dad's new OnCore ball."

"Is it legal?" Jamie wanted to know.

"Of course, Jamie. It was approved by the PGA last year."

Again, Brandon did not comment on his drive, but he was pondering the strange feeling he had in his body just as he had struck the ball. He had been playing with OnCore balls now for about a year and they did seem to go a *little* father and straighter, but that drive had been very different. Since he couldn't make sense of it in his own mind, he decided to let it drop. He did not need any BS from his friends. When he left the tee box he spotted his dad outside the ropes and walked over to him.

"Did you see that drive, Dad?"

"It was incredible, "B". How did you do that?"

"Oh, I was using your ball, what did you expect?" Brandon quipped.

They both laughed and Brandon walked away still in a state of amazement. A sports reporter caught up with him as he made his way to the 3rd tee.

"Hey Brandon, I was standing nearby where your last drive landed. I have followed you on the tour for a while and don't remember that you ever hit a ball 315 yards. What was different with *that* drive?"

"Wish I could tell you, but I agree, I don't think I have ever hit a bomb like that in my life."

"Well it is noteworthy. Hope you hit some more like that in the next few days."

"Me too!" With a slightly noticeable pride in his step, Brandon caught up with his two friends.

\*\*\*\*

It was that moment when I realized that I had come to The Masters to live out a fantasy that was not realistic. In the back of my mind I had always thought that if…if I had not been afraid of the risk, years ago, I was good enough to have truly earned a spot in this tournament. But of course that did not happen. Hell, I was dead as a doornail.

Integrity, both personally and in business had always been part of my character. And now, even as a spirit, I would never do anything during the four day tournament to alter the outcome. However, playfulness had also been part of my character and I saw no harm in messing with a few of the players' minds during the next two days of practice. That would be flat out fun. So I noodled on a number of ideas that would get these boys chattering with each other.

****

As the resident ghost of **this** tournament, I recalled all the stories about ghostly sightings of Clifford Roberts over the years after his death. And thought this could be a perfect way to get a buzz going in the 2014 event. Roberts and the famous course designer, Bobby Jones co-founded Augusta National back in 1933. Roberts had the reputation of running the club as a 'benevolent dictator' for over 43 years. It was rumored that he provided significant funding for General Eisenhower's presidential run and because of that friendship Eisenhower made Augusta National his "Southern White House." (That was the next building where I would do a self-guided tour.) Despite Eisenhower's position as Commander in Chief and President of the United States, Roberts did not defer when it came to Augusta National. At one particular board meeting held during Eisenhower's presidency, he made a motion that a large Loblolly pine tree on the left side of hole #17, be cut down because Ike's 2nd shot frequently bounced off that tree. Clifford boomed that Ike was out of order, adjourned the meeting and stomped out.

So with all the Clifford Roberts lore connected to Augusta National, I could just see the headlines in the tabloids and had to chuckle. "CLIFFORD ROBERTS' GHOST SEEN AT MASTERS TOURNAMENT." This would take the starch right out of the collars of those snobby green jacket guys.

With a little experimentation, I found that a light spray of water wouldn't penetrate my invisible being, so this gave me an idea. That night just at sunset, workers were busy tidying up and preparing for the next day's crowds. The 18th green had taken a beating that day in the unseasonably warm April. High above that final green sat the tower from which the media filmed the final shots. A dim light from this tower lighted the green. I levitated just above the green and when the mist from the sprinklers hit me, the outline of my body became visible. I saw two women on the cleanup crew who were headed my direction. They were occupied chatting and laughing with each other. As they passed the green and approached the club house facilities, they noticed me levitating above the green. Screams of hysteria broke the silence of the evening. They dropped their overflowing garbage bags and raced toward the club house.

Two security guards rushed to assist. The ladies were interrupting each other babbling about what they had seen. My appearance couldn't have been more auspiciously timed as it happened that a local newspaper 'stringer' had trailed behind his fellow reporters and heard the commotion. He could smell a story and headed to get the details. Finally the women calmed down enough to tell a coherent story about a ghost levitating above the green. The security guards, who were exposed to all sorts of hijinks during the week, listened but skepticism was written on their faces. As the reporter approached, the guards' focus changed.

"Hey buddy, the course has been closed for hours. We are going to have to escort you out."

As the two guards reached to grab the report by the elbows, he hollered over his shoulder that he would pay the ladies for their story if they would meet him outside the gate.

Just as I had predicted, the front page of the local tabloid featured the two women with an artist's rendition of a ghost levitating over the 18th green. The headline read: 'Cliff Roberts' Ghost Spotted at Masters Tournament'.

Knowing the ghostly tales of Roberts' prior appearances, the ladies swore they had seen his ghost. In reality, it is doubtful they would even know what Roberts looked like. This "sighting" fueled additional reports of Roberts' ghost being seen. Within the next two days, copies of that tabloid were sold out in every newsstand and grocery store in Augusta and as far away as Aiken.

I was successful. My 'appearance' had created a stir among the golf world. Jokes would become common place before the tournament was over on Sunday and would continue throughout the season at Augusta National.

\*\*\*\*

Wednesday was the final practice round before actual competition began on Thursday and the crowds grew larger each day. I wanted to think some of that was my doing...but probably not; as difficult as tickets were to get. With no more hijinks planned, I wandered over for my tour of the Eisenhower cabin and found a spot where I could lay down. It appeared that the cabin had several bedrooms and two baths surrounding a large gathering room. I settled in for the night on one of the comfortable couches in the gathering room. There I found four gentlemen in conversation. Again, I eavesdropped and found the discussion fascinating. These four men had been coming to The Masters for many years.

They were members at Augusta National and each had held CEO positions before retiring. I was in awe, just listening to their exchanges. My rung on the corporate ladder was the one on the bottom, never having achieved more than sales manager of a small regional company.

As I referred to earlier, one very famous aspect of this prestigious tournament was the simplicity of the menu provided for spectators. The sandwich choices were limited: pimento cheese, chicken salad, minced BBQ or egg salad. Each sandwich came wrapped in green paper, matching the paper cups. At noon I meandered around the long lines and wished I could take just one bite.

On Friday morning, I made my way to hole #16. This was my favorite hole, because in 1986 I had witnessed Jack Nicklaus birdie the hole enabling him to win his sixth Masters. I roamed through the crowd, heading towards a Par 3 hole to watch the action. Since I could position myself anywhere I damn well pleased, this was the best Masters I had ever attended. It seemed that no matter what hole I was on, one obnoxious jerk followed me. He had a habit of shouting "GO IN THE HOLE, GO IN THE HOLE!" I figured it had to be the same guy. How could there be more than one obnoxious guy with such a booming voice? As I pondered what it must be like to compete in this amazing event, I caught a distinctive and familiar accent. The more I listened, the more familiar the voice became. I knew that voice! It was my good buddy, Ron Yatsko from Lake Keowee. As I turned toward him, I saw that the other three were also my Keowee Key buddies: Peter, Art and Geoff. These were the very same guys who visited me at the mausoleum. If a ghost had the ability to feel emotion, that was what I was experiencing. If I could have shed tears of joy, it would have been a soggy mess. My instinct was to rush over and hug each of them, as I had many a time in the past. Ronnie had always been good natured and I enjoyed his sense of humor even when we argued politics. Seeing them, I momentarily forgot about following Bubba. I could think of nothing more fun than to follow these guys around the course. I tried to think of a way to let them know that I was with them that day. Right now being a spirit was depressing me, because I could not share this experience with my best buddies. Perhaps being with my best friends was really the fantasy experience I was supposed to have. Well, so be it! Messing with Ronnie was something I had always done, so that came easy. I moved over beside him. They were all standing up against the rope near a par 3 green. I moved very close to Ronnie's left ear and blew into it twice. His reaction was comical. His head jerked and he blinked his eyes, as if to say, "What the Hell was that?" Then he looked around to see who was close enough to do it. He must have decided it was his imagination, as he turned back to watch an incoming golf ball. Then, I moved to the opposite side of Art and blew into his right ear twice. Art's reaction was predictable. He threw his right hand up to his ear and looked around to see what was blowing near his head.

"What's wrong?" Ron asked Art.

"I think a pretty girl just blew a little puff of hot air into my ear."

"Oh, man! You are delusional!" Ron retorted, not willing to admit he had felt the same puff of air.

"Hell, no I am not delusional. I'll bet you never had someone blow air into your ear, have you? I tell you that is what I felt."

Feeling guilty, Ron admitted: "Well, to be honest, I just had the same sensation myself. Happened twice!" This was more fun than levitating for the clean-up crew!

As it happened, the foursome my friends were watching included Brandon White. I had taken a liking to this young man and was disappointed to see him take a bogie on 16. My buddies decided to follow the foursome to the #17 tee. This hole was named Nandina. Brandon walked out and placed his ball on a tee. His routine was to tee-up, then back away from his ball, take a sighting and then a practice swing. He walked back, addressed the ball and did his final club waggle. I knew that with his score, making the cut on Friday was impossible, so I saw no harm in assisting him a little on this drive. When he addressed his ball, I took the opportunity to immerse myself again into his body to maximize his drive. White's normal swing rate was around 112 mph. So, when he reached back with his club behind him and his left shoulder planted firmly under his chin, both of our hands were on the grip. Together we made a 140 mile per hour swing. Geoff was standing between Art and Ron. He let out a long whistle, as he watched White's ball rise up and clear the Eisenhower tree. It continued with a slow fade, following the fairway as it bent right. Those familiar with the course could immediately tell that White's ball had just flown 340 yards. Several hundred fans witnessing that drive, expressed loud approval with their applause. Joe, who was following his son from hole to hole, called out to Brandon.

"That was one hell of a drive 'B'. How'd you do that?"

"Don't know dad. But we can talk about it after my round."

As Joe would surely tell friends later, his new OnCore golf balls should get some of the credit.

Now Brandon only had 90 yards to the hole. If he could make this a birdie, it would be his third of the day. Unfortunately, he made par.

****

White was good, but he needed more experience. I just liked the way he handled himself. So I didn't see any harm in giving him a little help on the final hole. This 465 yard hole was named 'Holly'. The fairway bent slightly right as it sloped up a tree-lined hill. The view of the hole from the tee box looked extremely narrow. All golfers could see from the box was a massive white sand trap on the left lying in wait to snatch their ball. To successfully maneuver this fairway, a golfer would have had to hit the ball 335 yards, to clear the trap and that had *never* happened. If the ball landed in the sand, hitting a wedge out of the trap and onto the green was almost an impossible fete, because of the elevation of the bunker. Most seasoned pros avoided the long drive, not wanting to chance pulling their ball into the trees on the right that stood like outfielders eager to reach out and trap it in the pine needles below.

Many young golfers, playing in their first Masters, panicked on this final hole, as thousands of eyes watched and second-guessed their every move. The most famous finishing hole in the world could turn a good round of golf sour.

So as White advanced toward the tee, I followed him, again sliding myself into his form. From his reaction, I think my intrusion gave him a strange sensation. Of course he would write it off later to the 18th hole jitters. Brandon knew that he needed at least 335 yards in order to clear the monster sand trap on the left. I could sense that he was lining up to hit the ball towards the trap. With my hands also on his grip, I felt him open his club face just a bit in order to make his ball fade away from the trap as it approached. Brandon, like most golfers, knew they could not clear that trap, so they tried to stay to the right. No one watching would have predicted what happened next. After doing his waggle, he made a text book back swing that only the young and trim could ever dream of doing. I did not need to help him do that. However, I took my grip inside his hands and by using all my strength, I followed through with him and together we made solid contact with the ball. Brandon's finish was 'world-class'. His club head completed its mission up and around the back of his head, and on up behind him. He froze in place as he watched the ball. It was a flight of beauty to see this ball in slow motion. The orb climbed slow and steady, delaying its descent until well passed the infamous sand trap. White felt a flush of pleasure as he handed the club to his caddie. How in the world had he hit a drive so far...again? That was three in one day!

As they approached the ball, his caddie confirmed that White's drive had exceeded 358 yards. As he strategized his second shot, he glanced back down the fairway. A 358 yard drive on hole #18 at The Masters...what a dream come true. Possibly a record. Now he needed a good finish. The hole was 107 yards away. This was his third season on the pro circuit, so he was used to the spectators, but never had he seen such a crowd. It was a good thing there was nothing in his stomach, or he might have lost it, just thinking about his final shots. His caddie, Jack, realized this was a once in a life time moment.

"O.K. Brandon, don't let this hole psych you out. Take several deep breaths and let's concentrate on getting your ball on the green. The pin placement today is below the mound that crosses two thirds of the green. As I see it, you have two choices. One is to aim just below the hole and putt up to the cup. This eliminates the breaks. The other choice is to hit the ball above the hole and let it make a slow role back toward the cup."

"Jack, you have more experience at this than I. What do you recommend?" Brandon asked.

"I would opt for the second choice and hit the ball above the hole, but the choice is yours, my man. I would also recommend using your sand wedge. Hit it high and it should just drop, without a big roll."

White took the proffered sand wedge from Jack and lined up for his shot. He was very comfortable with the wedge and was confident he could drop it onto the green...just how close to the hole, he was not sure. I decided he did not need my help with this shot, so I floated up to the green and waited for his ball to arrive. Suddenly, I realized that helping Brandon make this birdie would actually be living out my fantasy in a way I had not expected. No matter where it landed on the green, I would be there to assist.

Anyone who had seen Whites' drive on #18 was now watching his next shot with rapt attention and even the Golf Channel was providing live coverage. "In the first three days of this Masters tournament, this 358 yard drive is definitely unexpected from this young professional", offered Dan Hicks.

"I agree, Dan, said Jim Nantz. "Brandon White might be one to watch in the future. Unfortunately, I think this drive is too little, too late for Brandon this year. Even an eagle on this shot wouldn't be enough for him to make the cut. But, given that this is White's first Masters, even if he doesn't finish in two, his drive on 18 will be remembered."

White hit his wedge behind and under the ball, creating a big divot. It flew high in the air, just as he had planned. With adrenaline coursing through his veins, he worried that he may have hit his ball too far. He watched it land 8 feet above the hole on the top edge of the down-slopping ridge.

I was already there waiting to see where it would land. The ball, as predicted by Jack, dropped and looked like it would come to a dead stop. White had started his walk towards the green as The Golf Channel camera zeroed in on the ball. So this became my chance to give White a tiny bit of help. I dropped to my knees and with a flick of my index finger moved the ball just enough to start it on a slow roll towards the hole.

By this time The Golf Channel announcers were going bananas, describing in minute detail what everyone watching could see for themselves. The crowd collectively took in a deep breath as the ball continued its slow roll towards an eagle. When it sunk into the cup, the crowd erupted with deafening cheers.

The announcer was attempting to be heard over the crowd. "Regardless of how The Masters turns out this week, the eagle just made by Brandon White, will be not only be the shot of the day, but most likely the talk of the tournament."

****

I had remained on my knees as the ball went into the hole and the fans were going wild. I gazed around at the fans and fantasized that it was I, who had just made that eagle here on #18 of The Masters.

White and his caddie Jack were both stunned as they stared down at the little white ball lying inertly in the hole. Fans were still cheering as a reporter was attempting to get White's reaction.

At that very moment, a deep voice bellowed from directly behind me. Knowing that I was invisible, I did not think these remarks were being directed at me. The man with the brash voice repeated his comments.

"Just what in the Hell do you think you are doing? Hey, I am talking to you!"

Slowly I turned and stood. I looked into the face of an elderly well-dressed man who appeared to be in his late seventies. He sported a dated tweed jacket and a straw hat, whose style was decades old.

It felt like this man could actually see me. But if he could see me, he must be a ghost himself. He barked at me again as I was struggling to get my voice.

"Answer me! Why are you on this green messing with the golfer's ball? Don't you know that is unethical?"

The tone of his voice caused me to bristle. "Well I suppose maybe what I just did is not quite right. On the other hand, the boy was not going to make the cut and that was his final hole. I don't know who you are, but maybe you would be well served if you just minded your own business."

"Anything that happens on this course IS my business and always has been. I created Augusta National, and the kind of thing you just did could change the outcome of our tournament. I WILL NOT allow you to continue, so get off this property."

His tone was really pissing me off so I looked him directly in the eye and retorted, "I have just as much right to be here as you do. And I'd appreciate you not following me around like you own the place."

"Well, well, well. A man with guts! I like that. What's your name?" the man asked.

"Jason McNeill," I proudly responded. "And who the Hell are you?"

The man just laughed. "I'm Cliff and I'm guessing we are the only two on my course who can see each other."

Oh shit! I was standing face to face with the infamous Clifford Roberts. Now, I understood that his crusty reputation was well earned.

However, he surprised me. There was a slight change in his tone when he asked me, "So, McNeill, what brought you to Augusta?" I thought perhaps he was glad to have another 'spirit' to talk with.

"Well, I always loved to play golf when I was alive and fantasized that someday I would be good enough to play among the best golfers in the world."

"But you are NOT playing golf. You ARE interfering with the minds of these young players and changing outcomes. That is still not O.K. in my book. So, stop it or leave!"

"With all due respect, Mr. Roberts, I don't feel that I have changed any outcome of the tournament. That young man just made an eagle. He was not going to qualify for the weekend and all I did was give him a little confidence and his 15 minutes of fame. Because of my action, I think he will go on to be a much better golfer in the future, so your heavy-handed attitude is a little out of line." I actually surprised myself with this response.

"You are probably right." Roberts admitted. "This course and tournament were my babies. It was the most important part of my life and I let nothing get in my way." With a little pride he admitted, "I even ramrodded my agenda down the throats of the board...even Ike himself."

I really had overstepped my bounds by helping Brandon, so I promised Mr. Roberts that I would behave myself if he would just let me stay.

I wanted to catch up to my friends before they left for Lake Keowee and since I was being bold anyway, I suggested we might talk again tomorrow. Roberts made a slight nod and strode off the green.

It was getting late in the afternoon and I knew Art, Ron, Geoff and Peter would probably be leaving soon to go back to Keowee Key. As only a spirit can do, I searched the throng of spectators for my friends. I figured they'd hit the gift shop for some souvenirs before heading out the gates. I was right. I spied Ronnie talking with Art near the hat rack. Art had always been a big spender and had selected 6 hats to take back to friends. I really loved these guys and I felt infuriated that I could not make direct contact with them. However, I did have the ability to move objects. So feeling mischievous,

I slipped my hand into Art's pocket and lifted out his wad of cash. I slipped it into Ronnie's pocket. My next move was to lift Ronnie's money clip. He never carried much cash, so I knew there would be less than $50 inside. Then I slipped it into Art's pocket.

The fun would erupt when they checked out. I was delighted when I noticed that they were directed to separate cashiers at opposite ends of the shop. When it was Ronnie's turn at the register, he reached into his pocket and a puzzled look came over his face as he pulled out more cash than he had probably seen at any one time in his entire life. The stack of one hundred dollar bills was big enough to choke a horse. I watched as Ronnie stared at the roll of bills. Then slowly, he rotated his head around the room, covertly checking to see if anyone was watching him. Now he checked his other pocket, presumably for his money clip. I knew Ronnie suspected someone had set him up to take the fall as a pick pocket. While this was going on, across the room of wall to wall shoppers, Art had reached for his wad of cash to cover the $180 in Masters' hats. What he found was a money clip with fifty dollars and a credit card. Normally a self-confident guy, Art's face became flushed and he looked confused. Predictably he checked his other pockets...to no avail. Art looked at the young women and admitted, "I'm sorry, but I forgot something." I sat on top of one of the registers with full view of both situations and busted my ass laughing. Art got out of line to gather his thoughts. He looked at the money clip again and then the credit card and realized it belonged to his friend Ronald Yatsko. I could read Art's lips: "Shit! How in the Hell did I get Ronnie's meager money in my pocket? And, where the fuck is my money?" It was then that Art saw Ron heading in his direction.

"Ron, I have your money clip and my money is missing. What the Hell did you do?"

"Hey buddy, I have your wad of cash, but I have no clue how it got there. Here." Ron shoved the cash at Art, a little irritated at being accused. "You know me well enough to know that I didn't take those bills out of your pocket. But, I could ask you the same thing. Just how did you get MY money clip and card?"

They exchanged bills and as the heat of the moment subsided, they pondered, "How in the Hell did that happen?"

Still chuckling, I was sure they would be trying to figure this out for years to come.

That was such fun; I decided I was not finished with my mischief. I wandered into the gift shop office. No one was behind the desk so I took a pen and scribbled on two yellow Post-it Notes. I found Peter and Geoff sitting on a bench outside the shop waiting on Art and Ronnie. I folded the

Post-it Notes and placed one in each of their pockets. If I could only be with them when they found these messages and compared notes.

\*\*\*\*

It was already Friday. This week was flying by. Each evening I lay on the sofa of the Eisenhower Cottage, passing the night in a dormant state. My mind just shut down for eight hours and as the sun rose, so did I. Of course I had no need to eat or drink, but the smell and thought of coffee accosted my senses every morning. I still didn't know what would happen if I consumed a dark-colored liquid like coffee. I didn't want to risk that potential situation, so I abstained as everyone else enjoyed their morning joe. I decided to head up to the club house. It was going to be a beautiful day and the member and guest buffet breakfast was being served on the front lawn of the club house. The scene was one of a Paris street café with The Masters' green and white umbrellas and colorful spring clothing of the diners. Breakfast had always been my favorite meal and the best I could do was to inhale the aromas. The reality of finding myself here in the midst of living people made me feel sad that almost no one living today would have my same experience. As I floated among the diners, looking for faces I recognized I noticed an empty table in the corner set for four. The sign read 'RESERVED FOR CLIFFORD

ROBERTS'. Everyone knew he had been dead for years. Why would they reserve a table for him?

It was not long before I discovered the answer to this question. I started to walk away, but something made me turn and look back at the reserved table. Now, there was a man sitting at the table with his back to me. I moved closer and found that it was Roberts. He was just sitting there just gazing down the 18th fairway. I stepped closer and offered a, "good morning."

Roberts looked startled, but he recognized me immediately.

"Well, Mr. McNeill, I would have expected you to be back in Greenville by now."

"No, I'm here for the week. I want to hang around and see who will wear the green jacket on Sunday. I'm sorry to have disturbed you. I noticed that this table is reserved in your name. Not to offend, but since everyone knows you've been dead for years, what's the deal?"

"Even a reprobate like me earned respect for what I'd accomplished, so this table is always reserved in my name. When I was alive, I made a habit of taking my breakfast at this table every morning during The Masters. They have continued that tradition and it means lot to me." Roberts's chuckled as he continued: "Of course they don't have a clue that I actually sit here every year during the tournament."

Roberts offered, "Have a seat. I am expecting an old friend, but he sleeps later than me, so I always have to wait for the ol' bastard."

Now any friend of Roberts would also be a spirit like the two of us. The irony of that thought bumped my funny bone.

Although curiosity was killing me, I didn't ask whom he was expecting. I figured he would either tell me or I'd find out when the friend arrived. We fell easily into small talk. He told at length about how he and Bobby Jones had decided to build this course in Augusta, Georgia. He had not yet completed the story when his guest appeared.

As the man approached, he greeted us. "Good morning gentlemen."

Roberts spoke first: "'Bout damn time, Mr. President. Let me introduce you to another old buzzard, Jason McNeill. In his lifetime, he was from Greenville, just north of here."

My mouth dropped open. I was face to face with none other than President Dwight D. Eisenhower. I moved to stand, but he motioned to me, "Please, stay seated." He reached across the table and shook my hand.

Working hard to find my normal voice, I responded, "I am honored to meet you sir." Feeling the momentary silence went on longer than it probably actually did, I felt compelled to make conversation. So, stupidly, I asked him if he came to The Masters every year.

"Oh, wouldn't miss it for the world," he responded. "Other than being back in Kansas with Mamie, this is my favorite place in on earth. With that familiar smile on his face, he continued. "Of course if it had not been for my good friend Cliff, The Masters would not exist. I guess we have to give Bobby Jones a little credit as well. Don't we Cliff?" Roberts grinned and responded, "Hell, no!" He did concede slightly by adding,

"Well, this golf course would have never been built without Bobby, but the tournament is ALL my doing."

Ike shook his head. "Cliff, I never met anyone who ruled with a heavy hand like you did. You'd have made me a good general. As much as I got pissed at you, I always respected you for making this club the best known course in the world."

I had been so star struck by meeting President Eisenhower that I had not taken notice of his attire. Ike had been buried in the OD-green 'Eisenhower' jacket that he had made famous. Four of his medals were attached. But what really caught my eye were his pink trousers. At the same time, he took notice of my pink linen coat. We both burst out laughing and The President said, "Hey, if you let me borrow your pink jacket, I could have a pink suit."

"With all due respect Mr. President, I would not be comfortable posing as a general." Both he and Cliff roared in laughter at this. I was in awe of this man and felt a little uncomfortable being so casual with him, but it was really great to have someone to talk to.

Ike asked, "So what brings you down here from Greenville, Jason?"

"This may sound a little funny to you, but after they laid me to rest in the mausoleum, I discovered a cocktail party the residents held every Thursday. In conversations with several folks, I heard about something called 'fantasy trips'. I could get permission from the tomb gatekeeper to live out a fantasy as long as I was back within my allotted time. Like you Mr. President, I played golf all my life as an amateur. But my dream had always been to come to Augusta and play as a professional in The Masters. So now after death, here I am trying to take it all in before I have to return Sunday night."

Roberts broke in to my narrative. "Ike, you would not believe what I caught this ol' buzzard doing on Friday." I knew what was coming next. Roberts had a smirk on his face as he continued. "Friday, I was down by the eightieth green watching to see who might qualify, when I saw Jason out on the green messing with one player's ball. He hit a nice approach shot, but it was not close enough to make the hole. Jason here, tapped the ball and it rolled toward the hole, before a very enthusiastic crowd and it dropped in the cup, giving this kid an eagle. As you can imagine, Ike, I gave this guy holy hell!"

Ike cocked his head and looked at me: "You really did that?"

"I confess. I did."

A slow grin spread across Ike's face, "Why would you do that Jason?"

"Well, the best way I can explain it is that it's really boring to be dead." Ike roared and I continued, "I know I'll never again be able to enjoy the benefits of living. But, by assisting that young golfer, who by the way was not going to qualify anyway, I felt that it would inspire him and let him understand that anything is possible. No harm was done by this action. Brandon White got his 15 minutes of fame and I had a sense of gratification from being a part of that. I think you might both agree, it's no fun taking long naps in that very confining putrid box."

"You don't have to tell us about that." Ike looked at Roberts and laughed. Roberts agreed, "You got that right! The one thing I hate is having to wear these damn out-of-style clothes. They are beginning to age and one of these days they will rot off me. Then what will I do?"

"I guess you will be walking around 'necked', Cliff." Ike said. Roberts persisted, "Beats the Hell out of me why someone felt it necessary to throw my straw hat in the casket before shutting the lid. I always hated that hat!"

Roberts's sudden wit was breaking me up. Nothing ever written about him indicated he had a sense of humor.

Ike added, "Do you think I like wearing this green jacket and these pink pants to The Masters every time I'm here? Mamie wanted me to be buried with the medals on my lapel along with my favorite putter. What about you Jason? What's your story about the pink coat and jeans?"

I am sitting here in amazement that these great men are conversing with me as an equal. I was still in high school when Ike became President.

I feel embarrassed as I gave my reasons. "I died on the golf course from a heart attack. Shortly before, I had attended my 60th high school reunion. When I was in school, we didn't have the money for fancy clothes. In order to earn money, I drove the school bus. Guess I wanted to let people know I'd been successful, so I went all out. I spotted this pink linen coat and the rest was history. When I died, my buddies pulled the outfit from my closest. And here I am wearing it until, like Mr. Roberts said, it rots off my body. No one threw in a hat, but each of my golfing buddies dropped a golf ball in my casket. And one Jackass told everyone that the balls he brought were all found in the woods and they all belonged to me."

The three of us sat there under the umbrella for what must have been two hours and talked mostly about the current tournament and some of the people that both Ike and Cliff had known in the past. There were many things I would love to hear Dwight Eisenhower talk about, but that could wait.

As we rose from the table, Ike was very gracious. "We will be here again tomorrow morning Jason, if you care to join us." I was delighted to accept his invitation.

\*\*\*\*

When I was alive, it was customary for the four golfing buddies and their wives to gather at the Keowee Clubhouse for drinks. Ronnie, Geoff, Peter and Art had returned from their day at The Masters with a number of funny stories, including the one about how Ronnie and Art got their money mixed up. The retelling of it must have been hilarious. It wasn't plausible that they had picked each other's pocket and how would a pick-pocket benefit, if there was nothing missing from their wallets? Peter had a shocker of his own, but he wanted to wait until he could get the others away from the crowd before he shared what puzzled him.

"Hey guys, I had a weird experience too. I haven't told you yet, because I needed time to think it over and make sure I wasn't going crazy. You know I'd had a few beers that day." This revelation brought uproarious laughter from the other three. Peter *never* had just a few beers.

When the laughter died down Peter continued, "When I cleaned out my pockets, as I do every night, I laid my cash on the dresser. Stuck to my money was one of those yellow sticky notes. I didn't remember having any reason for sticky notes in my pocket, so it roused my curiosity. I unfolded the note and about fell over." Peter paused and let the 'reveal' hang in the air a while.

"Come on!" Ron asked impatiently in his whinny northern twang. "What did it say?"

Peter's face was now a flushing pink. He reached in his pocket and without a word he merely put it in front of Art's face and then Ron's and finally Geoff's. As each man read the note, incredulity grew on their faces. "What in the Hell is this?"

What they were reading was the note I had slipped into Peter's pocket in Augusta.

After an uncomfortable silence, Geoff finally admitted, "OK, I was not quite ready to share this, but I found one just like that in my pocket too." He reached into his wallet and produced the note. The two notes read exactly the same. "I really miss you guys" and the notes were signed, 'Jason'.

All four just stared at each other. "It can't be!" exclaimed Art, the most pragmatic one of the four. "But it sure looks like his signature," offered Ron. "Hey guys, I know this feels like some kind of hoax," added Geoff. "But, I have one of the books that Jason wrote. He signed it for me and last night I compared the two signatures. I'd swear they're a perfect match."

"But it is just not possible" Art exclaimed, again.

Ron blurted, "This is crazy. I mean Jason has been dead now for, what, a year and a half?"

A mischievous smile brightened Geoff's face. "You know, we each experienced something that none of us have answers for. I may be a little open minded, but I have never believed in the paranormal. Still, you have to admit this is off the wall stuff."

Just about the time Ron opened his mouth to make another comment, Jan, always the life of any party, laid her hand on Ron's shoulder. "You boys look way too serious for a Friday night cocktail party at the Club." Ron opened his mouth before he thought about what he was saying. "Oh we are just talking about a ghost. I mean Jason McNeill."

"What about Jason?" Jan asked.

"Oh, we just always think about him when we play this course on Fridays."

Jan had come over to let Ron know that she was heading to the house. She pecked him on the cheek and bounced off. Once out of ear shot, Ron whispered, "I know I said 'ghost', but how else can we explain this?" None of them wanted to admit that they believed in ghosts or spirits.

****

Back at Augusta on Saturday morning I rose from the couch in Ike's cabin where I had again reposed for the night. During this fantasy outing, I came to learn that one's olfactory glands must still be active in the spirit state, as I caught the aroma of freshly brewed coffee coming from the kitchen. I was looking forward to joining Ike and Roberts again at their designated Clubhouse table. Roberts had already established that Ike was not an early bird, but evidently neither was Roberts, this morning. So I wandered unseen among the living as they enjoyed breakfast. I spied Brandon and his dad talking with several others. As I predicted, Brandon had not qualified for the tournament, but was still entitled to Clubhouse privileges for the weekend.

I floated closer so I could eavesdrop a little. This was becoming a new favorite pastime, I realized. Wish I'd had that ability when I was alive and in business. I could have made a killing against my competitors!

As I had suspected they were rehashing Brandon's eagle on hole #18. It was featured on the Golf Channel as the 'shot of the day' and would turn out to be one of the most talked about shots of The Masters that year. His amazing drive would go down in the record books as the longest drive on hole #18 at Augusta National. That next morning at the table, sporting a wide grin, Brandon pulled from his pocket, the ball that he had used.

One of the young men at the table asked, "May I see that ball?" Brandon handed it over to his friend Paul.

"OnCore" Paul read aloud, "Never heard of it before. Where'd you get it?" Brandon extended his hand toward his Dad in a gesture that allowed Joe to promote the unique ball his company invented. As President of OnCore Golf, Joe did not miss the opportunity to champion the innovative technology of his company's golf ball.

As I turned to continue my roving among the tables, I noticed that Ike and Cliff were now seated at their special table, so I headed over to join them.

"Good morning Jason," greeted Ike. "Take a seat and join us."

I couldn't help thinking about his accomplishments: West Point grad, five-star general, President of the United States, and the visionary of our interstate highway system. And here I am, sitting and visiting with him like we were next door neighbors.

Roberts interrupted my musings, "Who are you going to follow today, Jason?" I admitted I was going to follow Bubba Watson during the afternoon. "You like Bubba," Roberts asked?

"I really like to watch him play and I admire the man, too. He's kind of a loner and appears to be very down to earth. I remember reading that after he won The Masters a few years ago, he took his family to the Waffle House for dinner. Now, that's my kind of guy!" Ike laughed and said he had heard that as well.

"Jason, you seem to be very engaged in this game," Ike noted.

"As I told you yesterday, Mr. President, my dream had always been to make it on the circuit. When I was in my early twenties, I carried a 4 or 5 handicap. Friends and a few pros encouraged me apply for qualifying school, but I was a newly married man with a family and I just couldn't ask them to make the sacrifices that would be required."

We discussed the tournament and the potential winners for a while and when I sensed a lull in the conversation, I decided it was time to excuse myself, and allow these two old friends to reminisce in private. Ike graciously invited me to drop by the Eisenhower cabin around six. He said there would be someone else I might like to meet, but stopped short of sharing who; piquing my curiosity. We parted with handshakes and like a breeze I drifted toward the first tee.

Nicklaus, Palmer and Player were standing there together, basking in their notoriety. I hovered near them, again, so I could practice my eavesdropping skills. Evidently Player had been standing near hole #18 when Brandon made his eagle.

"I mean, it was the two most perfect shots I have seen in a very long time. I actually knew that kid when he was about 6 or 7. His dad was president of my company for a few years."

Bubba was up next and all conversation stopped as we followed the flight of his ball. I felt a strong urge to fly beside it and aid its flight. But I knew Roberts would be hot on my trail, ending this enjoyable week. So, regretfully I decided I had better satisfy my urges by merely walking beside Bubba and his caddie. I loved to watch Bubba hit his driver. As a lefty, his drive was unique and he had such a natural swing. Part of my infatuation with this athlete was that he had such natural talent and his success had come without ever having a lesson.

Despite my decision not to change the outcome of the game, I was itching to have a little fun with Bubba. He was slated to tee off first. As he stood next to his caddie, discussing his approach, the caddie reached for the driver that famously sported a pink club head. I had to be quick with my mischief. As Bubba removed the head cover he noticed that this was not his driver.

"What the hell?" He turned toward Scott, with frustration on his face. Scott looked as surprised as Bubba.

Then an "oh, shit" from the other player's caddie made them both turn to see the pink driver revealed in his hand.

"Man, I have no clue how this happened," apologized the other caddie, "But it appears you have **our** driver." They exchanged clubs, and I was satisfied with my antics as laughter broke out among patrons close enough to witness the mix up.

It was well known that Bubba was a loner and tended to be sensitive. As I watched his face, I knew he wondered if this guy had perpetrated this trick to unnerve him. However, being the professional he was, I watched his face quickly transition as he concentrated on his first drive.

****

As promised, I arrived at the door of the Eisenhower cabin promptly at 6:00pm that night, still intrigued by Ike's evasiveness about the other guest. Figuring that even as a spirit, it would not be proper to just float in, I rang the doorbell. Moments later the door swung wide and Clifford Roberts invited me in with an exaggerated gesture.

"Come in." Roberts sported a broad grin, not his normal countenance.

"I'm honored to be here," I told Roberts, still feeling a little intimidated. The rich hardwood floors were covered with beautiful oriental rugs, bordered by two massive leather sofas.

Roberts directed me toward the bar where Ike was making himself a scotch on the rocks. "Welcome, glad you took me up on my invite and dropped by," Ike greeted me.

"What would you like to drink Jason? I always liked to keep a very well-stocked bar."

I selected my usual vodka tonic. As Ike fixed my drink, he quipped, "Normally I like a little branch water with my scotch, but tonight I am going to take it straight." Not being familiar with that phrase, I asked Ike, "Branch water?" Ike laughed, Oh, I forgot, how much older I am than you. That is an old name for stream water added to a drink. Being from the South, I was sure you'd be familiar with that phrase!"

With a drink in my hand, I decided to check out the photographs and paintings in this opulent room. Suddenly Ike appeared behind me. "Let me tell you about my collection."

Ike and I made our way around the room. Most of the photos were Ike's family and friends. I was familiar with the photo of him sitting behind his desk in the Oval Office. Next to it, hanging over the fireplace, was a painting of his grandson.

"Jason, Mamie and I moved around a lot during our military days and then after the war into the White House. During those years we lived in a lot of houses, but never really had a home. This cabin was the closest we had to a real home, for us both. I spent a lot of time here playing golf or bridge depending on the weather. Here, I was surrounded by my gang of friends. There was privacy and security during a time that we needed both. We could let our hair down.

"Did you say hair?" piped in the familiar voice of Clifford Roberts. Ike shot him a sideways glance and retorted, "Well you know what I mean, Cliff." Then, turning back to me, Ike continued. "As annoying as Cliff could be, he was a major player in his day and a major factor in my presidential campaign. Cliff put up his own money and organized a support team dedicated to getting me the Republican nomination. Behind that gruff exterior, Cliff is a very generous man and a true gentleman. That old SOB turned out to be one of my very best friends."

Listening to Ike's stories, reminded me about my childhood. I was a very young man when Ike was President and could remember the sacrifices civilians made during World War II. I could remember my father telling about when President Truman and General Marshall appointed Dwight Eisenhower as the Supreme Commander of the

Allied Forces and under his leadership Germany and Italy were brought to their knees.

Ike and I moved from the main room into the kitchen. I could hear a commotion at the front door as it flew open. A loud voice carried throughout the cabin. "I told you I would return." This brought an uncharacteristic frown to Ike's face and I heard a low groan, "Oh damnation!" I wasn't sure if this entrance brought friend or foe!

Then a man with a sharp nose, a tropical worsted military uniform that sported five stars pinned just above his pocket, entered the kitchen.

"Mac, 'bout time you got here," Ike greeted.

"Can't be a proper gathering without me can it?" retorted the guest.

"Oh, Hell! Jason, you probably won't remember this old warhorse. But he was the nemesis of my entire military career! General, this is my friend Jason McNeill."

Suddenly recognition dawned, and again I was filled with amazement. I extended my hand and said, "Of course I remember you General MacArthur. You were a real hero during my early school years."

Ike grumped, "Don't inflate that over-active ego any more than necessary, or Mac will become even more intolerable than he already is." MacArthur's reply sounded like 'harrumph' and then he barked, "Ike, where is my drink?"

"You still drinking Manhattans?" Ike's naturally gracious nature reappeared.

"I do, and when you were my lowly assistant in the Philippines, the only reason I kept you around was that you could make good Manhattans."

"You were the general's assistant?" I asked in amazement.

"Oh ya. It was back in the 1930's, but this bastard was a hard man to please even then," Ike retorted.

MacArthur hooted, "You were wet behind the ears, just out of West Point and damn lucky to train under me."

"Well, you must have done an excellent job General, because I ended up as Commander In Chief!" Ike countered.

"Ya, ya, and you wouldn't know it but I came to your funeral, just to make sure you were dead. Have to admit though, that they did you proud. It was a classy affair."

"And I came to yours", Ike retorted, "but just out of curiosity. And it was so typical of you to dictate that it be stretched out to a seven day affair! That's two days longer than a State Funeral. Just a little obsessive wouldn't you say?

I mean they had to haul your ass all over the east coast before they planted you in Virginia."

MacArthur, beginning to feel the heat, deflected the attention to me and asked why had I come to The Masters? So I retold the story about my love affair with golf.

"Well as you can guess" the General said: "Anyone who stayed in the Army as long as I did, played a lot of golf. When I wasn't killing Japs in the Pacific, I always played the base courses. Hell, I was never any good, but that didn't bother me! A great diversion, it was."

"Jason, if you are a student of history, you'll remember that Mac got his butt kicked in the Philippines and his parting shot was the same threat you heard at the door a few minutes ago: 'I shall return.'"

Not to be outdone, MacArthur decided to end this discussion. "Well I did tell them I would return and when I did, I kicked the Japs' damn asses." So here I am."

Ike responded to my question about whether he had played golf in the military. "Hell no! I was doing grunt work in the Philippines while Mac was obsessed with photo ops, pretending to be walking knee-deep in water on the beach in his freshly pressed kakis."

Despite the barbs, I thought that these two must have been good friends. However, what I would learn later was that Ike had never really liked MacArthur. He couldn't tolerate McArthur's vanity and penchant for theatrics. Ike, being the gentlemen that he was, avoided bringing up the fact that MacArthur was eventually fired.

The four of us settled on the large leather couches and I just sat quietly listening to their conversation. What an opportunity this was, hearing the old war stories, first hand. They went on for hours and suddenly it dawned on me, that we should have seen the other guys that were staying here. When I mentioned this, Roberts answered that they were most likely out for dinner and we would need to clear out before they returned.

I knew that Ike had been the one to recommend a small pond be built behind the cabin, so I decided to ask him about it. Reportedly, he had been an avid fisherman. "Mr. President, have you dropped a hook in 'Ike's Pond' lately?"

"I have, but it's been a couple of years and it was a mistake I don't plan to repeat!"

"Why not?" I queried.

"Well I was having a good day and landed several nice sized bass. I pulled them up on the bank, intending to release them. But unknown to me, someone witnessed me landing a couple of fish. Of course, no one could see **me** pulling them in. The man went unhinged and ran to find his buddy to show him that fish were flopping up on the bank by themselves. Now realizing the stir I had caused, I put the fish back before he returned, and the guy looked like an idiot. I have not fished down there since."

About 10:00pm guests staying in the Eisenhower cabin began to return from dinner. So, the four of us decided to wander over to the 'Little White House', located above the clubhouse pro-shop. It had served as Ike's Augusta office back when he was President.

Ike sank into the same old leather desk chair that had served him well many years ago. None of us seemed ready to end this congenial gathering, so Roberts and I encouraged MacArthur and Ike to share war stories...of which there was an endless supply.

The tales of WWII adventures were still being told and disputed by these two veterans when I noticed that the sun was peeking through the window. Never had I experienced such a night. Making the moment particularly poignant, was the realization that this was Sunday morning at The Masters and that meant the tournament was coming to a close. Soon, I would have to head back to my tomb in Greenville. As I was fixin' to depart, I thanked each of these remarkable men. Eisenhower, McArthur and Roberts, all had their names engraved in history. Me? I was just a name on a bronze plate that covered a crypt. But, oh, what stories I would have to share with my Tomb Society friends!

So, I took my leave in order to have the full experience of Sunday at The Masters. They wished me well and invited me to join them again in future years. You can bet I'll ask Wally for that privilege!

****

Sunday afternoon at the 2014 Masters, was a year at Augusta National that would be recounted in clubhouses around the world as golf enthusiasts remembered Bubba Watson's amazing finish. The term 'Bubba Golf' was coined after this tournament. And I was here to see it live!

I enjoyed the morning roaming around the course taking in the sights and sounds exclusive to The Masters in Augusta, Georgia,

One location I had not yet checked out was the media area. Today, as it had been for years, CBS's Jim Nantz led the play-by-play. Jim brought class to the broadcast booth. Traditionally, he invited guests to join him. Their chatter back and forth brought the tournament to life for millions of viewers at home. That morning, as I stood in the booth, Nantz was summarizing the previous three days of golf. As we know now, it would turn out to be an unforgettable tournament. At 2:30, the official starter on hole #1 announced Louis Oosthuizen and Bubba Watson's names for the final paring of the day. I floated into the closed studio set and took one of the celebrity chairs that stood empty. In the seat next to Nantz, sat Tom Watson. This year Tom had not made the cut so was available for Nantz's celebrity appearance. At that moment on the first tee, all eyes were on Bubba and Oosthuizen. Fans obediently remained silent until each player executed their first drives of the day. Nantz reflected on how Ossthuizen had won the US Open in 2010, and had high hopes of being the second South African to win The Masters. Nantz also noted Bubba was there hoping to win his second Masters tournament. I wasn't sure I liked the way Nantz was talking about Bubba's opposing personalities. According to Nantz, "one minute Bubba could engage with the fans in a goofy way, endearing him to the spectators. The next minute he was so focused on his game that he ignored everyone except his caddie."

 I sat there watching the giant monitors and listening to Nantz and Tom Watson and decided to give Nantz a scare. The sun was at such an angle that it reflected everything inside the reporting booth onto the tinted window. This made it possible for the two men to see their own images reflected in the tinted glass. Nantz glanced at the window and did a double take before recovering his composure. When the station broke for commercials, Nantz confessed to Watson, "Man, I must be losing it. I'm seeing things."

"Well, you're not the only one, Jim. I could swear I saw a man in a pink sports coat in the seat next to me," Tom agreed. With that confession, they both glanced over and the empty chair...and saw nothing.

I had to laugh at this and knew it would bug these two guys every time their paths crossed.

****

Well, having had my fun in the broadcast booth, I decided to follow my hero. It was the last day of my fantasy adventure. Although my experience had been very different than what I had expected, it had been a truly amazing week! I had been able to experience the game of champions up close. I hovered at the tee box as the best golfers in the world made unprecedented drives. I squatted on the greens to predict the path of the ball as they drew on their skill to sink putts that most of could only dream of.

As Louis and Bubba walked down the first fairway, I studied their expressions. For them, the world did not exist beyond the hole they were playing. I watched Louis quietly conferring with his caddie about distance and approach and the important selection of clubs. Conversely, Bubba remained deep in his own thoughts. At 4 shots behind Louis, coming into this round, I could see he was frustrated. Over the years that I had followed Bubba, it seemed he could always forget the previous hole and play as if this shot was the first of the game. As I joined him to walk down the first fairway, I could not help but notice his body language. He had a very regal posture and he sported just a little swagger in his step. The stance, the swagger and the concentration on his face gave Bubba an air of confidence. He was in a zone. I was no more than six feet from Bubba and couldn't help wondering what it would feel like to *be* him. Playing this 'out of body' fantasy was the ultimate. I could understand why Eisenhower came back every year. I never did remember to ask Ike how *he* was able to leave Kansas and make the trip every year. Did his resting place have a weird little guard at the gate like Wally? Did they have a Tomb Society too? Maybe because he had been President, he just moved about as he pleased.

Like all Bubba fans, I groaned when he bogied the first hole. I mean this was Sunday and now he was 5 shots behind

Oosthuizen with seventeen more to play. I could see his jaw tighten, transforming his youthful face. Given the way Louis had been playing recently, and knowing Bubba's unpredictability, Bubba fans were beginning to sense that Louis Oosthuizen would end up as the 2014 Masters Champion. A 5-shot lead seemed almost insurmountable. Then Bubba's birdie on Hole #2 expunged the bogey on the previous hole. Bubba had narrowed the lead by one stroke and hope returned to Bubba fans.

Anyone who has watched a bowl game and seen their team come from behind, understands the sense of exhilaration as the tide begins to turn. That is just how we felt when Bubba made birdies on holes number 2, 5,13,14,15 and 16. For all golfers, but especially for Bubba fans, this was golf at its very best. The crowd noise erupted at Hole #15 to a volume usually reserved for the winner on Hole #18. Still walking beside my hero, I watched Bubba's enthusiasm become palpable. As each of the three succeeding holes ended in a tie, the possibility of a playoff became a reality and every fan on the course moved in to surround Hole #18. It would be the first hole of a sudden-death tiebreaker. It was a 465 yard par 4. As I stood there next to Bubba on the tee, I could almost read his mind. He had a par on Hole #18 in both his first and second rounds and made birdie on day three. His par on #18 today ended regulation play with the expected tie and ensured a sudden death playoff.

Bubba knew he had the strength to fly his ball over the infamous sand trap on the left that loomed at 335 yards, but not wanting to risk landing his drive in the deep trap, he would maneuver his ball toward the center of the fairway. This year the trap had been extended 5 yards closer to the center of the fairway which caught a lot of players off guard. I moved onto the 18th green and waited for their second shots to land. For me, there was no greater joy than immersing myself into the middle of this historic moment.

Louis's second shot was away, so he approached his ball first. I felt, as much as observed, the sea of humanity encircling the green. Other than the green and the fairway, every inch of grass was occupied by a fan. The sinking sun created a picture-perfect setting. Among the spectators, I spotted Clifford Roberts, glowering at me. His head was shaking back and forth in warning. But I had learned my lesson. I would not touch anyone's ball and would not influence the exciting outcome of this event. I also noticed Brandon among the crowd. He stood with several other amateurs that had missed the final cut. I could sense that someday this young man would be among those who vied for that green jacket and hoped that I would be here to cheer him on.

The suspense built as Louis missed his putt for a birdie. If Bubba could again birdie this hole, it would be over. His putt came within inches of the lip, continuing the tie. Now, everyone charged toward Hole #10. The scene was like Wildebeests stampeding across the grassy plains of Africa!

Bubba was tall. Dressed all in white, he loomed above the crowd, strutting toward the 10$^{th}$ hole, oblivious to the 'herds' around him. This, 495 yard par-4 hole was considered the most difficult at Augusta National. Every golfer's dream was now being played out. Bubba still had the honors and set up to make his drive. His adrenalin was barely under control.

His secret weapon in winning this sudden-death match was his legendary explosive swing. His biceps tensed as he gripped that pink-headed driver. It was launch time folks! The safest approach was to aim his drive just left of fairway center. A long line of stately evergreens guarded the fairway's right side, taunting contenders. Anyone who has ever gripped a driver in competition knows that when under pressure, your natural tendency is to over-swing and pull a shot. Bubba was no exception. When Bubba connected with the ball, it was obvious he was going for a long drive, fading to within 145 yards of the green. As his ball soared, a low moan rose from the spectators. The ball hooked back into the trees on the right side of the fairway. For those watching Bubba's reaction, he appeared stoic, but I was close enough to catch the momentary expression of disappointment. This drive must have eaten up his gut.

    I quickly moved ahead of him to survey the damage. Debatable if you could call it luck, but his ball dropped behind the fans, in an open circle of pine needles. The only thing you could see from the ball's lie was a small parting of the trees straight off the fairway. The green was hidden around the corner to the right. Broadcasters and spectators alike assumed the only option was to chip it back onto the fairway. Oh, no...not Bubba. Not Bubba Watson. When it came to creative shots, no one held a candle to him. Well, maybe no one except Phil Mickelson. I stood in front of him at the edge of the trees so I could see its trajectory. Bubba contemplated the shot for what seemed like hours.  He requested the 52 degree wedge from his caddie. When the ball released, I swear, once it cleared the trees, that ball made a 90° right turn and dropped on the front of the green rolling towards the hole. Nervously, I looked quickly around to see if Cliff Roberts was anywhere in sight.  That ball traveled at such a weird angle, I was sure ol' Cliff was gonna' accuse me of meddling.

Bubba had two putts left to win. He missed the first, but made the next one, to win his second Masters Tournament! You didn't have to be as close to him as I was to observe the tears streaming down his face. He moved toward the fans, found his Mom and gave her a huge bear hug. Then Scott got the same form of thanks. We had witnessed one of the most incredible finishes in the history of golf. I was dancing around the green like an Irish leprechaun. What a finish to my fantasy week! To be right there on the green for those final shots!

I made a bee line for the awards ceremony and stood right next to the podium. A familiar presence on my left turned out to be Ike. "You know Jason this was always the best part of The Masters."

When Bubba was handed the mic, his remarks did not surprise me. He humbly thanked God, his family and his friends. Over the years, Bubba has admitted that he deals with demons at various times, but today, there were no demons...only spirits standing beside him.

As I stood there watching the crowd lugging chairs to their cars, I was flanked by my two new friends...Ike and Cliff. How could I convey the importance of this experience for me? I knew I would never play in The Masters as a contender, but this was so much better! The time had come for me to depart.

## Back to Tranquility

As the sun ducked below the horizon, leaving a trail of brilliant orange, I plodded toward the entrance where seven short days ago I had materialized in front of Augusta National Golf Course.

Twilight was creating a veil of silver over the brilliant orange sunset. Soon the moon would begin its lazy rise from the east. By this time the parking lot was deserted.

According to Wally's instructions I did not have to be back to the mausoleum, before midnight, so I took one final look around, committing to memory all the sights and sounds of the week. On the trip home, I knew what to expect, but it still gave me the heebie-jeebies remembering the nauseating tumble through the ether.

Just as quickly as my conveyance had begun, I found myself standing at the front door of my mausoleum in Greenville.

I heard a 'click' and reluctantly drifted through the open doors. Once inside, the doors snapped shut behind me. "How was your fantasy trip, Jason?" I turned to see the familiar face of Wally, the gatekeeper. That unattractive face bore a grin that made me feel at home.

"Oh, you have no idea!" I said. "When I was alive, it would have never been possible to experience The Masters as I just did."

"Well, it's good to have you back, Jason. I am sure after your exciting week you will need some rest."

I did not want to go anywhere else in the tomb, but directly into my casket. I knew I would miss some of the Thursday night socials, but there would be plenty of time in the future.

## Months Later

I don't know how long I had been in my casket, but it had been long enough! Time to socialize! I knew it was April when I returned from Augusta, but had no clue how long I had isolated myself. As I wandered the circular hall, I noticed what looked like Christmas cards wedged behind plates on some of the crypts and beautiful poinsettias on the floor. Well then...it must be December.

Vince was standing against one of the crypts and greeted me with a smile. "Hey, you've been quiet for a long time, buddy. I don't think we've seen you since your fantasy trip to The Masters." I returned his greeting with a friendly slap on the back. "No, I don't think you have. Vince that was definitely a fantasy experience. Even you won't believe my stories."

"Well, Jason, it's party time in the back, so you'll have an audience for your tales. You always liked that! Let's go join the group for some Christmas cheer."

Trying to kick-start my humor for the stories I was about to regale the inmates with, I quipped, "I have been dying for a drink. "By the way Vince, remind me how we get booze into the tomb."

"That's always a tricky thing" Vince said: "We learned to watch ol' Roscoe, one of the grave diggers. Usually after sunset, he stops down at Howard's liquor store on Wade Hampton. Normally it is a Monday. He buys himself a bottle of Jack. Two of us follow him into the store. While he is there, one of us picks up a half gallon of Vodka and the other causes some commotion in the back room to distract the owner. We quickly sneak our booze out of the store and deposit the bottles in the back of Roscoe's truck. He carries more trash and crap in the bed of that truck than you can believe. And that includes his 'empties', so disguising our bottles is never a problem. He has a little shack near the mausoleum, so we can easily remove our stuff from the truck when no one is looking. Once we observed some kids with mischief on their mind in the cemetery and gave them the scare of their lives when they saw bottles floating in the air toward the mausoleum." Vince chuckled and added, "I bet they would never tell that story, do ya' think?"

I had to laugh at this. Vince had always been a funny guy and it felt good to be in his company again. How I had enjoyed the famous corn beef sandwiches he served at Vince Perone's Restaurant.

"Vince, have *you* been on any type of fantasy trip since I saw you last?" "Oh yes," Vince grinned, "I took one to Italy a few months back. I had never been to my homeland and it was spectacular. They couldn't make deli sandwiches like I could, but I did enjoy watching them make pizzas. Wish I'd have made it over there when I could have enjoyed all the food!"

"I know what you mean. There was so much booze at The Masters, but I was afraid to try anything that wasn't clear!"

As we rounded the corner, I spotted all the regular suspects, plus a few new faces. It usually saddened me to see new people in this place. I was greeted with a lot of: 'How you doing?' and 'Where in the Hell have you been?' Those who remembered I had ventured on a fantasy trip wanted the details. So, here was my podium for the stories I always liked to tell. I launched into how I met President Eisenhower and General MacArthur. Of course, the golfers in the group wanted to hear about Clifford Roberts and Bubba Watson. With a drink in their hands, everyone paid rapt attention as I spun my tales. I don't think the three vodka tonics had given me a buzz, but getting together and enjoying their company sure did!

There was a big crowd at tonight's party...everyone still in the same attire. That probably bothered the ladies more than it did us guys! But it was what it was. The volume of the conversation escalated as residents joined the throng. I guess everyone wanted to hear my stories...or at least that is what I told myself. Suddenly, an unmistakable voice rose above the din. "Hey Jason, you ol' turd." Before I even turned I knew that it belonged to my old classmate, Dan. "Hey Dan, when did you arrive?"

"Oh, I kicked the bucket about two months ago, so here I am good buddy." He made his way over to me and greeted me with his signature slap on the back. In fact, his nick name had always been 'slap-a-back Dan'. With that, you'd think he had been a politician, but Dan had owned the most successful real estate company in the Upstate. And it was so, because Dan always made people feel good. He had that uncanny ability to make you feel as if you were the most important person in the room. I saw that he hadn't lost that touch!

"Well, welcome to the Tomb Society. I hate to tell you, but most of the real-estate in here is already sold and there are never any resales." Dan burst into one of his infectious laughs.

"Hey Jason, you've been here a while, who in the heck is that really weird guy? I always see him near the doors."

"Oh, the one with clothes that looked two hundred years old?" Dan confirmed my assumption with a nod.

"That's Wally," I explained. "I don't know much about him, but if you want to leave the tomb, he's the guy that grants permission."

"Damn," Dan said. "I had no idea you could ever leave this morbid joint."

"I can assure you, Dan, that it is possible. I recently returned from a trip to The Masters." I beamed proudly, anxious to regale Dan with my escapades.

Some days later, remembering Dan's interest in Wally, my curiosity piqued as well. So, one evening after dark, I stood right at the front door. Any movement around those doors brought Wally's immediate appearance. He emerged from the shadows with a very friendly greeting

"Good evening Jason."

"And good evening to you, Wally."

"It's really cold out there tonight and looks like we might see snow. Were you thinking of going out?"

"Not tonight Wally," I said. "Just wanted to visit with you. Tell me, I'm curious about how you have this position as gatekeeper at our tomb?"

As I waited for Wally to respond, I noticed more closely his clothing. His coat and trousers were extremely threadbare and my first impression of him as a character out of a

Dickens novel, remained. His coat hung around his knees. There were four button holes but only one button remained, and that hanging by a thread. Both his top hat and shoulders were coated in dust. It was as if his entire being were in a rapid state of decay. The skin on his face and hands resembled that of an elephant and the dreadlock appearance of his hair hung around his yellowed collar. When he spoke it was through an accent I could not place.

"Well," he paused for a long minute. "Jason, I don't usually share, but if you want to hear it, I will tell you. Many, many years ago the Cherokee Indians vacated the land around here, to the white man. In 1777, a little village was formed about 3 miles west of here, called Pleasantburg. You would know it as Greenville. In 1831, my family and I escaped the famine of Ireland and we settled here. My father had just enough money to make a down payment on some land suitable for farming. We had been potato farmers in Ireland, so it was natural that we do the same in Pleasantburg. Our farm numbered two hundred acres. It was good beyond our belief for a while, but then the fever hit and I lost several brothers and a sister and finally my whole family. I was the last to die, but not because of the fever. But I am getting ahead of my story. It was the practice back then to reserve a scenic spot on the farm for a family cemetery. One by one, every one of my family was laid to rest in our cemetery." I could hear the sadness in Wally's voice as he told of his family's tragedy.

"With the fever came bad years of drought. It was like Ireland all over again. We were cursed! Then the local leaders put a tax on our lands. My father had no crops, he had only me to work and we could not pay the tax." I could feel bitterness in his voice as well, now.

"In the end, just like in the motherland, we lost everything. A man offered to buy our land, but paid my father almost nothing. My father was very ill by this time and the only thing he wanted was for me to be taken care of. I was allowed to live in our family house until I died and then I was to be buried with my family in our cemetery.

"As I lay dying in the old house, I felt the same 'out of body' experience that you had. For a very long time this grip of purgatory has imprisoned me somewhere between life and death. To be honest, Jason, I'm tired. I want to go on over, whatever that brings."

I had not been prepared for this sad story. It was obvious that all of this happened to Wally and his family over 200 years ago.

"Wally, I'm so sorry to hear about your family's difficulties." It seemed he to need to share his life story, so I stood quietly and continued to listen.

"Eventually our family farm fell into ruin. The fields were overtaken by trees and literally became a forest. Many years later, a local builder heard about an old pile of stones in the woods almost concealed by underbrush. He wanted these stones for a grand house he was building. Jason, those stones were our grave markers. My family's names were lost to the erosion of time. One day the builder brought a wagon and two men. The theft of those headstones had obliterated the only record of my family's existence. Today they remain as part of the foundation of a Greenville mansion.

My gut wrenched with grief for this old soul.

"The bitter-sweet truth of why I am here," continued Wally, "is that in the 1930's a wealthy family bought the very land where our graves had been located and ironically, they made it into a public cemetery. Now after only 70 years, it is almost full."

Thinking that I already knew the answer, I still had to ask, "So, where is that cemetery Wally?"

"Jason, we are standing on the exact site where my family and I were buried. This mausoleum covers that grave site and the bodies of my mother, my father, and all my brothers and sisters lie beneath us."

I jumped as if I had stepped on someone's head. "Right here?" I exclaimed.

"Yes, right here, Jason. With the grave stones taken, the plat showing the land, never indicated a small family cemetery."

"My God, that is one of the most tragic stories I have ever heard. That makes sense why you are here with us, but how did you come to serve as our gatekeeper?"

"Being the last family member to pass, I took it upon myself to become the family's sentinel. I will make certain my family's graves are never again desecrated. And, I have come to feel a kinship with you all and in a way responsible for the souls that are suspended in time. Not sure why, I just do."

I knew Wally had shared a very private part of himself and vowed to keep his confidences to myself. But, if only the living in this community could learn of the injustice done to these Irish immigrants!

## Return to Keowee Key

It did not take long for me to become bored again. The Thursday night cocktail parties were no longer all that interesting. Only when new residents joined us was there any news. Resting in my coffin seemed to take up more and more of my time. I was not motivated to get out of the box and move around and talk to people. I think it must have been three years before I felt awake and energized again.

Curiosity drove me into the halls to see if anything had changed. Of course, it had not. Predictably, there were a few new names on the formally unoccupied crypts. I half-heartedly attended the cocktail party on Thursday night and as I meandered among the party-goers my thoughts wandered back to Keowee Key. The memories of my last home made me want to venture out for another fantasy exploit. Like a bolt of lightning it hit me, I wanted to go see my buddies in Keowee Key. If I missed anyone in this world, it was those four guys who had meant so much to me in the latter years of my life. I missed the comradery and especially the pranks. It has been so much fun to mess with them at The Masters, especially because they could not mess with me. That was a rush!

It was spring, just like it had been 3 years ago when I traveled to Augusta National. I knew they would be out playing golf on Fridays. Probably on the very golf course where I'd had my heart attack. I knew it would take guts go walk back onto that course, but that was the level of my friendship with these guys.

That night I decided to find Wally. As predicted, he appeared from the shadows when I approached the doors. "Mr. Jason, I have not seen you for a very long time."

"Guess I took a little nap. But now I'm feeling kind of restless, Wally."

"So, you want to head out on another trip, Jason?"

"Was it that obvious?" Wally merely grinned.

"Wally, I am thinking that I'd like to take a trip to Lake Keowee. I had some very good friends there and I really miss them. Don't need a week out, maybe just a couple of days."

"I can arrange that Jason, but you must know that you will be setting yourself up to be unhappy. You will not be able to talk with them, or show yourself to them."

"I understand. But I just don't see any benefit in lying in that damn box day in and day out. I know this purgatory time will come to an end and the only hope for me is that, despite my pranks, I will end up in heaven. I just feel that judgement day for me is a short time coming. So I want to take advantage of these fantasy journeys while I still can."

"I see you have your heart set. When do you want to leave?"

"My friends always play golf on Fridays so I'm thinking I'd make the trip this next Thursday night so I'd be there first thing Friday morning. I'll be back by Sunday night."

\*\*\*\*

At 4:00am, I stood at the tomb's front door. Because of my past trip to Augusta, I already knew the routine of transporting my spirit through space and time and arriving at my chosen spot. I felt Wally's presence next to me and he gestured toward the doors. Once outside, I turned back to see Wally fading into the shadows and felt a pang of sadness for this odd little man.

Once outside the tomb doors, I closed my eyes and allowed my arms to hang loosely beside my body. My concentration zeroed in on the first hole of the Keowee Key golf course. Early that morning, I found myself standing on the first tee. The sun was just rising and the first golfers would not be teeing off till after 7:00am. If I had been visible, passersby, seeing me in my pink linen coat and designer jeans with no shoes, would have assumed I overindulged the night before and lost my way home. These images made me laugh.

As the sun rose above the horizon to greet me, I deposited my spirit on a nearby bench and recalled the 12 great years spent in this retirement community. It had been a wonderful place to spend my final years. Always something to do! A successful salesman must be comfortable with people. My personality had been a perfect fit for sales, so when I retired, the social scene came naturally.

I knew this golf course like the back of my hand. I must have played it a thousand times. Even with my eyes closed I could envision the bend of the first fairway and how it dipped as it neared the green. If your adrenalin got the best of you on this hole it could be a disaster. The morning dew blanketed the grass as the hum of mowers could be heard near the maintenance building. Cart boys were arranging the golf carts in orderly rows and placing placards above the windshield, identifying each twosome. Fridays were always popular and members filled up the course. The group I had played with would probably be in the first group out. It had been nearly five years since I played my last round with these guys. The best part had always been that you never knew when you were going to be messed with. Some of our player's handicaps were questionable and in that crowd it was not unexpected! This group of guys still had testosterone flowing through their veins, so winning was a big deal, even if the prize was only $10 bucks.

It was finally 7:00am and the old bunch began to wander in. Some headed to practice tees and others to the putting green. I got excited as I spotted my friends. This would be a couple of very happy days. Because there were 16 in our group that played on Friday morning, I wasn't sure that my 4 buddies would be a foursome. So, I was delighted to see Geoff and Ronnie come to a stop at the first tee in their cart, and right behind them were Peter and Art.

The average score of the five of us had wavered between 87 on a good day and 100 when we shot crappy golf. Today my plan was to make my four buddies look like pros. I wanted it to be a round of golf they would brag about for a long time. The competitive rules set up by this group of 16 dictated that there would always be 8 winners (the lowest scores) and 8 losers (the highest scores). The best part of these rules was that the 8 winners each bought a pitcher of beer and the 8 losers drank for free. Everyone put $5 in the kitty, so the eight winners divided up the $80 dollar pot.

Wahoo!! Rehashing our game became a loud and boisterous activity.

As a rule, golfers who play together frequently can be ruthless with each other. The bantering increases with each hole and becomes even more vicious at the Turn House Grill after the game. It must be a guy-thing when giving each other crap all the time can bond you together forever.

So here's the deal with Geoff: On some days he is a pretty good golfer. He has good distance on his drives and can sometimes get on the green in regulation. And when he's having a good round he is 'Mr. Personality'. But, when his round is ugly, riding in the same cart with Geoff, is just not fun. Bad goes to worse and balls end up in the woods or the lake...I think, on purpose. On rare occasions, his clubs get slammed to the ground. On those days we called him 'Skippy'. Sometimes we would bet if we were going to be paired with Geoff or with Skippy. Geoff always took this ribbing well. Today, if I had anything to do with it, the guys would definitely not be playing with Skippy.

Now Peter is one low key guy! That is, as long as he didn't run out of beer. Peter was a really decent golfer and he took pride in his game. While the rest of us admitted we belonged on the senior tees, Peter always played from the white tees. Despite constant ribbing about needing to be macho, we could never get him to the senior tees. He would just pop another beer and grin at us with that infectious smile.

Now Art, another reliably good golfer, claimed a 24 handicap and had sworn by that number for years. It always made him a favorite in tournaments! Each time he approached the tee box, I could predict his methodically slow process...always exactly the same. First, he would stand behind his ball and put the face of his driver on the ground to line up. Then he would make some adjustments and do it again. This habit brought either snickers or cajoling if we were in a hurry.

When I first met 'Icon Ron' fifteen years ago, I nicknamed him 'the most interesting man in the world' because I thought he looked like the bearded man in the Dos Equis commercial. That nick name stuck and he came to believe he truly was an 'icon'. Although the rest of us were up for a game in any weather, Ronnie was strictly a fair weather golfer. If it was too hot, he WOULD NOT play. If it was too cold, he WOULD NOT play. Whenever Ronnie approached the ball he looked down the course for an agonizingly long moment, visualizing his drive. Then he would look down at his hands, adjusting and readjusting his grip. We would all know that when he finally got around to his waggle, he was ready to drive.

I was jolted out of my reverie about Ron's approach when I overheard Art say that he missed ol' Jason. "Remember how he always told people he was 81. He had used that line for over 10 years. He really liked to use it on younger golfers, saying that maybe they too could hit a ball that far when they turned 81. What a joker! You know, some days he could pull shots out of his ass and then other days he was worse than all of us together. Sadly, he never got beyond 79."

I was thinking that this thing about me saying I was 81 had always been fun. It had made me feel good when someone would say, "Wow, you don't look that old".

\*\*\*\*

When Geoff set up to make his drive I floated up behind him. The first hole was 330 yards from the gold tee. As he did his waggle I immersed myself into his body. I could tell that Geoff was tensing up and his grip was just a little too firm. I think that when I invaded his body, he relaxed. I moved within his body as he drew back and with a very strong down swing, together we made contact. Ronnie, Peter and Art knew where a good drive on this hole should land. Geoff's ball just hung in the air and when it finally hit the fairway, it ran like a fox. It looked to be only 75 yards from the hole. Geoff smugly looked back to see if his buddies had witnessed his great drive. They had!

"Damn Geoff, how in the Hell did you ever hit that far?" Peter asked.

"Beats the shit out of me!! But I'll take it."

Geoff was filled with self-satisfaction and a grin on his face that went from ear to ear. His 'Skippy' personality was nowhere to be found.

Then I did the same thing for each of the other three. All four had hit the drive of their lives. Never before had any of them hit a ball 250 yards. Guys in their 70's just plain don't do that.

None of them needed my help to chip up on the green, so I left them alone. Icon and Peter hit their balls within ten feet of the hole while Art and Geoff were more like twenty feet away. I could tell by the smiles on all their faces that they were relishing those incredible drives instead of focusing on the putts they needed to make. Art's ball was near the back of the green with a couple of undulations between his ball and the hole. At 20 feet, he knew he'd probably end up with a 5 for a bogie. Art was an average putter, so you never knew. With this group, a par was considered a really good score.

"Hey, Arty, don't choke up now, cause you are putting for a birdy," Peter taunted.

Art always found comments like these unsettling. I could tell from his face that he wished they would keep their damn mouths shut for once.

"Yes damn it, thank you very much. I can actually count to three." This grumbled comment brought on chuckles from the others, who were delighted to know they had gotten under his skin.

I decided to move up close to the hole in a spot I figured Art's ball would come to rest. For the second time he lined up his putt and thankfully the peanut gallery stayed quiet. Art's putt was just a little hard. I could tell that it would be close to the hole, but probably roll a few feet further. As he watched the ball, Art was wishing it into the hole. At this point, I reached down when the ball was within inches of the hole and deflected it, so it just dropped in, nice and neat.

Art was ecstatic and threw his arms and putter above his head, displaying a couple of uncharacteristic jumps into the air. I wished I could describe the look on his face as it sunk in that he had made a birdie. That brought silence to the other three!

Geoff was next up. He was feeling pretty confident, still basking in that awesome 250 yard drive. But, being competitive, I could tell he was feeling the pressure to pull off a good putt. From where he stood, it was going to be a left to right break. Peter, Art and Ronnie stayed very quiet, not wanting to golf the rest of the round with 'Skippy'.

Geoff seemed unusually composed. He determined his line, drew back his putter about ten inches and made a beautiful smooth putt with follow through. I could see that the ball was going to be close, but it would miss by about eight inches. So as his ball rolled within three feet above the hole, I touched it gently with my toe. To everyone's surprise it looked like the ball had hit a divot and redirected into the hole for yet a second birdie.

"Holy Toledo!" Ronnie said. "Did you see that?"

Geoff didn't say a word, for fear, I'm sure, that he didn't want to jeopardize this streak.

Icon Ron was next to putt. From his position, the ball should roll straight. However, pulling to the right was one of Ronnie's weak spots. I didn't think he needed my assistance but was ready just in case. Ron seemed as cool and collected as Geoff had and the ball headed straight for the hole. Even when it looks like it can't miss, a ball will sometimes rim the hole and refuse to make the final plunge. Such was the case for Icon's ball.

"Well I'll be dammed!! Why can't I make a putt like you two guys?"

When Ron headed over to the ball to give it a tap in, I intervened and tapped it just enough to sink it. Cheers went up from all four of them.

Now the pressure was really on for Peter. Of the four, he was probably the most consistent putter. The other three remained quiet, not wanting to jinx this streak. If Peter could also make a birdie, it would be unprecedented. They were all high handicappers and the other players in their group knew it. The believability of these four guys making four birds on the same hole was nil.

Peter did not need my help. He dropped his ball in to make it four birdies. If these guys were enjoying their game today, I was having the time of my life. And despite what Wally told me, I felt like I *was* playing golf with these guys...in my own way.

When they were getting off the carts and walking over to the second tee Ronnie broke the silence.

"You know, I was just thinking. I wish ol' Jason had been here to see those four birdies."

That comment made me chuckle. It felt good knowing that they still thought of me.

Hole #2 two was 312 yards from the gold tees. It dog-legged about half way down a slope then bore right and upwards to the hole. There were some oak and pine trees guarding the right corner. These always tempted the long hitters who wanted to place it right in front of the green. None of us boys ever made that mistake. In this instance, we had known our limits. Most of the time, if the ball headed toward the trees, you were gonna have a bad hole. When that happened, they had no shot to the green. But today was somehow different. Each man hit his drive without hearing taunts or snarky comments from the others. After the success they had on hole #1, confidence was high.

Geoff was first on the tee again. I could tell he was thinking of driving his ball up and over the trees. He would definitely need my help to make this shot. So, once he addressed his ball I merged within him. I could tell he was tensing up to make a hard swing, so I gently caused him to open his club face just a little to keep him from making a hook. When he pulled his club back, I made sure that he kept his right arm and elbow close to his right side as he made his swing down, out and back up. The result was picture perfect. All four of them held their breath as the ball kissed a few pine boughs and dropped onto the fairway 45 yards below the green.

There were high fives all around. Geoff had never even tried this shot before.

"You know something?" Geoff said, "I can't explain it, but it is like there's an inner strength helping with these shots. It's weird!"

Now it was Art's turn on the tee. He was capable of hitting a ball as far as Geoff, but common sense dictated that he wouldn't risk landing among the trees. There were too many holes left. So he aimed his shot towards the left side of the fairway, allowing his natural fade to the right to work for him.

My intent was to help my friends have a game they would never forget, but not on every shot! I wanted their wins to be believable. Since Art had a good drive, I decided to see what he would do by himself this time. He drew back, made a nice smooth swing and hit his ball in the sweet spot. It did not go as far as Geoff's, but it did land in the middle and 75 yards from the green.

Icon was next up. He was by nature a conservative player and he countered that with usually being full of himself. When I was alive, I loved messing with him. Ron was thick skinned and could take my ribbing. He was also very good at giving me back a double helping of his Yankee bullshit. In his case, I chose not to interfere with Ron's drive either and he hit a nice ball in the center of the fairway within 100 yards of the green.

Last up was Peter. As usual he would hit from the white tees. That meant the difference was 21 yards. From that extra distance, his only choice was to hit his ball straight down the middle and reach the dog leg, so as to have a shot at the green. I knew Peter could make this shot, so I did not interfere. Peter was feeling confident and it showed when he hit a high ball straight to his desired target. Every golfer knows that if they can get a few really good holes early in their game, they can drop up to ten shots on the scorecard.

As each of them approached their ball, I could tell they sensed a great game ahead. Little did they know!

When they walked away from the second hole, each one made par.

I am not going to recite play-by-play for all eighteen holes but there are a couple more that have to be shared.

Hole #6 was the toughest hole on the course. From the gold tees it was 326 yards. With a well-placed shot, a golfer would land on the edge of a small pond that guarded the raised green. Between the pond and the green, a sand trap defended the front side. Near the pond, the fairway bent back to the right which blocked out a player's view of the green. This was a deceptive hole because the fairway was rather narrow. The right of the fairway was bordered by tall grass. If you missed your target and landed there, your only choice was to chip it back onto the fairway. That is, if you could find your ball.

Up to now the net score for my four friends was an amazing two strokes over par. They were on a roll, and I was delighted!

"What are you going to hit here, Icon," Art asked.

"Think I'll leave my driver in the bag 'cause I really want to stay on the fairway. My best bet is usually my ol' 3-wood for both distance and control. How about you?"

"I'm staying with the driver. I think I can hit my usual fade and make it work." Art said.

Peter was up first and hit a nice drive, leaving himself 145 yards to the hole.

Geoff was a little anxious and landed in some oak trees off the left side of the fairway. He had slammed the drive, so when it hit a tree, it bounced back out, it landed in the center of the fairway. Now, I couldn't take credit for that bit of luck!

"You got away with that one Skippy." Peter taunted.

"Wait just a minute." Geoff retorted, grinning. "Skippy is not playing today."

All four balls ended up in a good spot on the fairway that made good approaches to the green. I decided to see where the second shots would land. Icon was the closest at 138 yards, so he waited for the other three to hit. On his second shot, Art was about ten feet the left of the green and Peter was in the sand trap. Geoff chose the wrong club for his second shot and his ball came to rest on a little bank behind the green. None of these were really bad shots and with a well-placed chip, a par was still possible.

When it was Ronnie's turn, he'd had time to calculate which club he needed. He chose his 7 iron. It was his 140 yard club. Even though the hole was only 138 yards away, the green was raised so this club was perfect for that situation.

Ronnie's ball came in high and dropped at about six feet behind the flag. I let the ball roll up to my foot and gave it a little thump. It rolled back and dropped into the hole. There was a moment of total silence before the jumping commenced.

Art screamed, "It's an eagle, it's an eagle!" Geoff and Peter ran over to Ron, picked him up and began to toss him around. It took a minute to sink in that he'd actually shot an eagle on the number one handicap hole. Even though they'd all seen it sink, they all walked up to peer down into the cup. Sure enough the ball was snug and secure in the hole. Photos of the moment were made for bragging rights. Never in his life had Ronnie experienced the thrill of an eagle.

On hole #8, Geoff had a hole-in-one, to add to their combined success that day. This one he did on his own. I think I was not paying attention on that hole, because it was where my fatal heart attack had occurred. Not sure if it was a coincidence, but I once had a hole-in-one on that same hole.

They all knew that this round of golf would be unbelievable to the larger group of 16. So, they stopped under a tree after finishing hole #18 and double checked the scorecards. They had shot a gross 320 among them and when they subtracted their 91 combined handicaps, the net was an incredible 229. They were giddy as they headed toward the club house. I had assisted them on several holes, but their self-confidence had kicked in and most of their good shots had nothing to do with me.

Icon told Geoff, "I just cannot believe that all four of us played so far beyond our normal game. This is going to get belligerent in the clubhouse when Jim checks our cards today. I'm sure he'll figure we didn't really earn these scores."

"Well, let him have his rant." retorted Geoff. "We all witnessed each other's shots and not a one was even in question. But I'll bet you that two guys on the same team have never come into the club house with two eagles"

"Ya," chuckled Ronnie, "We'll make sure they all remember this round for a few years."

In the other cart, Art confessed to Peter, "There were times today when I felt like someone else was hitting my ball. I know it's weird, but sometimes I didn't feel in total in control of my shots…especially the best ones!"

While these guys were rehashing their game, before turning in their cards, I took one of the pencils from the cart and signed my name by the two eagles. Peter and Art had already signed their names as a witness, so no one had noticed my name on the card next to theirs. I could not wait to see what would happen when they noticed.

They posted their scores in the computer before heading to the Turn House Grill. Since they had been the first team to tee off that morning, they were the first back in. They eagerly took seats at the table always reserved on Fridays, for the sixteen friends.

I had enjoyed the 'settling up' process among the winners and losers almost as much as the game itself. Typically the more we drank, the louder we got. We laughed and ribbed each other to no end. It was a Friday ritual and I'm sure the staff at the Turn House Grill was glad when this rowdy group of 16 finally gave it up to head home.

I couldn't miss this part, so sat myself on an unoccupied chair next to the reserved table and soaked in what I had missed for the last number of years.

Geoff and the team knew they had to be winners so ordered their pitcher of beer, even before the rest came in. It was pure torture waiting for all the scorecards to be collected by Jim and posted. Neither Ronnie nor Geoff said a word about their eagles as others began to drift toward the table. They wanted to see Jim's reaction and hear him run his mouth, with that heavy English accent.

"All right mates," Jim bellowed above the din. "Let's have your cards, so I can see how badly I beat you low-lifes. First, two of you have not given me their five dollars! I only have seventy dollars so which of you two numb skulls have stiffed us?"

We all loved Jim's 'in-your-face" personality when it came to tallying up the scores. I couldn't wait to hear what he'd say about my four buddy's game.

Jim began listing the individual scores and suddenly shouted, "What the Hell!!" Gene, usually the low scorer, asked, "What's wrong Jimmy?"

"I don't believe this shit!! Geoff's team is claiming a net score of 229." Sandy, from the other end of the table, called out that it had to be a mistake and ordered Jim to recheck the numbers.

"Ok damn it, give me a minute and shut up! I can't think with all your noise."

Art, Peter, Icon or Geoff said not a word in their defense. They just sat with smug looks on their faces. When Jim came up with the same total twice, he shoved the cards to one of the others in the group and told them to check his numbers.

The total remained at 229. Jim looked hard at the cards to determine if mistakes were made.

"Wait just a minute. Icon did you actually have an eagle on hole #6?"

"Yes I did." Icon could not resist the big cat grin.

Then in unison, they all started yelling that Icon owed them a round of drinks that night at the club.

"OK, OK. You know that payback is usually reserved for hole-in-ones, but if you are in the bar tonight, I'll buy you dip-shits a drink." After the commotion, Jim continued his examination of the infamous scorecards.

"Now gents, if you think the eagle is a big deal, just listen to this! These guys all claim to have had birdies on number one. That's a crock of shit! It sure looks like these guys have taken to cheating." This brought out a roar of mock protest. Geoff, spoke up and said he would swear to it as unbelievable as it looked, they really did all have a bird on the hole.

"Oh, this just keeps getting better! Damn it Geoff, did you really have a hole-in-one on hole #8?"

"Yes sir, I did," bragged Geoff, as a smile as big as Ronnie's crept across his face.

By now other members that had been sitting outside the grill heard all the noise and came in to see what was going on.

It was then that Jim spotted my signature. "Who is Jason?"

Art responded, "What do you mean?"

"I just noticed that you and Peter witnessed Geoff's hole-in-one, but there is a third witness. Who the Hell is Jason. Looks like he witnessed Icon's eagle too. What are you guys up to?"

"Let me see that card." Ronnie reached over and grabbed the card. Geoff looked over his shoulder and responded, "I don't know who that is, but we've had the cards in our possession all day and nobody else had their hands on them."

Jim shot back: "The only Jason that I ever knew died about five years ago."

This was better than what I had hoped for. It was such fun to see all the uproar.

This mystery over the signature brought back an eerie reminder to Geoff of the time when he and Peter had found yellow sticky notes in their pockets, signed 'Jason'. He would definitely check the signature against the one on his scorecard. Peter was having the same thoughts. They exchanged a glance, but neither put words to their suspicions.

As the golfers began to depart, many of them stopped to remind Ronnie that he'd be buying drinks. I was sure Ron hoped that not all would come back to the bar, as Ronnie had a reputation for being a little on the cheap side. Since Geoff had a hole-in-one, maybe he'd share the expense.

Although neither had verbalized their suspicions about my signature, Art suggested they meet at the pool to compare signatures on the scorecards. When they got to the pool, Peter and Icon were there waiting as well. They set the scorecard on the table.

"You know something." Geoff admitted, "This look like the same signature to me. What do you guys think?"

They each took a turn at examining the signature and agreed that it had to be the same person who had signed the stickie notes. No one said anything for a few minutes. Then Art spoke up, "I really don't know what to think about all this but it's kind of like….Jason is here with us."

Icon made a weird noise as if he was agreeing he was afraid maybe Art was right. "How can we explain what's going on here?"

They sat there by the pool talking for almost an hour.

Not knowing what to do, Art suggested, "Hey guys, up in Salem there's a Fortune Teller and Psychic. I've seen her sign. Maybe we should take these to her and see what she says."

"O.K. hold on a minute." Icon shot back. "You are not suggesting we go see some old hag up in Salem about this? You can't be serious!"

"Well Ron, if you have a better idea, let's hear it?" retorted Art.

I would have never guessed that this could develop into so much fun. I thought about whispering in Icon's ear and make it sound like a voice from the grave. That would scare the living piss out of him. But I was too anxious to see how they would play this out on their own.

After drinking his last beer, Peter said he'd heard enough of this ghost talk.

\*\*\*\*

When Geoff and his wife came around the corner of the Keowee Club Bar that night, they were surprised by the crowd. There was no doubt that all 16 of the group had shown up for their free drinks. This was about to be a pricey bar tab, even if he and Ronnie split the cost. Several guys surrounded Icon and picked him up, holding him over the crowd yelling 'hero'. Geoff was not about to be grabbed by a bunch of drunks, so he climbed up on a bar stool, out of reach behind some of the women.

I moved around the party and listened in on the conversations. When I was alive, I had rarely missed these Friday gatherings. It was a great place to flirt with the ladies. Of course, Icon always though he was the most interesting man in the world and attractive to all women, but I knew I had given him a run for his money.

Jim had always been the loud mouth in the crowd. Tonight, sporting his prize red T-shirt with the Ferrari logo, he climbed onto a bar stool and clinked his glass to get everyone's attention.

"We have the pleasure tonight to be in the presence of two golfers who *claim* to have had eagles today. Of course we all question their veracity. But if they did fudge their cards, as you can see that lie is going to cost 'em bunch. So join me in a cheer, and then drink up! Hear, hear," he bellowed and everyone followed.

This was priceless to me. My expectations had been exceeded today. Since I couldn't visit with people as I had when I was alive, I wandered back down to the pool house. I had thoughts about checking out my old townhouse but decided against it because I remembered that Wally warned me this trip would make me sad. I changed my mind and decided to find Peter's runabout boat. It had a nice little cabin where I could spend the night.

Trying to hit all my old haunts, I headed the next morning to Sister's Restaurant in Salem. This had been one of my favorite places. Not surprisingly, my four buddies were gathered there for breakfast. They had 'Jason' signatures with them. The night before, they had scoffed at Art's suggestion to see a Psychic, but here, over breakfast, they decided that they had nothing to lose and they were always up for an adventure.

They piled into Art's car and headed up the road. I couldn't miss this one. To cover their nervousness they laughed about what an ill-advised idea this was. Among themselves they swore that no one else would ever hear about where they were headed. Ronnie laughed, "If what we are about do to ever got out, they'd call us a bunch of idiots." Nothing new there, I was thinking.

A few miles down the road they spotted a very small homemade sign near a rusty mailbox.

"There it is." Art shouted.

They turned onto a dirt road lined with tall weeds down the middle and on both sides. About a quarter mile on the road the weeds were replaced by tall pine trees and heavy underbrush. The rutted road ended at a dilapidated single-wide trailer. The rusty front door could be seen through a broken-down screen door which was hanging by one corroded hinge. The trailer at one time had been white, but now most of the paint had peeled away, leaving exposed sheet metal. Alongside the trailer sat an old Ford truck. Given the trash piled in the bed, it looked more like a trash bin than a vehicle. The windshield was obstructed from the inside by old newspapers and Styrofoam cups. The stoop in front of the trailer's door consisted of three cement blocks partially concealed by a dirty shag runner. When the guys stepped out of the car, a flock of crows made a racket as they scattered away.

Icon, being the most squeamish of the four, looked around, and whispered, "I am not sure this is where we need to be."

Geoff took leadership of this expedition. He approached the door, stepping gingerly on the filthy shag rug. The door had a tiny window that was clouded by a film of dirt. He reached through the broken screen and knocked on the door three times. Geoff wondered if anyone had ever ventured to this dump to get their fortunes told. He was glad it was morning. Being here after dark would be completely crazy. Gypsy's were all over the world, so could it be that one lived here in Salem and dealt with the Paranormal? Soon Geoff could hear movement and the door knob turned. An old woman's heavily wrinkled face peeked out at them. Supporting Geoff's suspicion that no one ever came out here, she asked in a scratchy, loud voice, "What do ya'll want?"

Geoff cleared his throat, "Well, we saw your sign out by the road and thought maybe you could help us."

"What is it you want?"

"Well, we think we've been getting some strange messages from someone who has been dead for almost five years and we don't know who to talk to about it."

"My place is small. Do you all have to come in?"

"Yes we do," stated Geoff very emphatically, knowing that he didn't want to go in that place by himself. Safety in numbers, he thought. "We are all involved and we all need to hear what you have to say."

The old women just stared at them for a moment. As Geoff was deciding that it might be wise to just to turn around and leave, she mumbled,

"I suppose you could all come in, but wait out here." Then the door closed with a rattle.

Not one of them had ever had their fortunes told and all they knew about fortune tellers was what they had seen in movies.

After what seemed like an interminable amount of time, the front door creaked open again. As they entered the trailer, darkness of the interior initially prevented the men from seeing details of their surroundings. Every window was draped with a blanket or covered with cardboard. It took several minutes for their eyes to adjust. In the center of the room, a space had been cordoned off to create a spot for her fortune telling. There was no crystal ball on her table, which surprised the guys. The air was rank with mildew. At the small space in front of her table she had placed three chairs and a small bench. Icon quickly took the bench. He was thinking that maybe the smell came from the ancient shag carpet which had probably never been vacuumed, but then realized it was incense she was burning. The only light in the room was the glow of four half-burnt candles. In total, the atmosphere was a little unnerving, even for me, the ghost!

A small framed sign sat on the corner of her table. It read:

Majilla
Professional Psychic
Your Fortunes Told
$25.00
Cash only

Hand written below the price was a scribbling that said "no guarantees". I cracked up. Her attire consisted of a plethora of gold bracelets, a silver head band that secured a black scarf around her head and a colorful, but tattered caftan. Her face was covered with a thick cake of foundation and way too much black around her eyes, which she must have applied while we were waiting outside. With the makeup and head scarf, it was difficult to judge Majilla's age. She perhaps was in her 70's, give-or-take a few decades.

Peter jerked as he noticed that she had the head of a dehydrated snake, some old bones and a few animal teeth lying in a dish opposite her 'professional' sign. This was going to make a great story when I returned to the Tomb Society. Once everyone was settled, she sat quite still staring at us through those sunken black eyes. About the time I sensed that Ronnie was poised to jump and run, she closed her eyes and began to sway, as if meditating. This performance made Art particularly nervous. Art was the intellect of this group (which didn't take much). He had more education than the rest of us and had traveled extensively. I could tell he was second guessing his suggestion that put them in such a ridiculously phony situation.

At last, Majilla opened her eyes and looked directly at Geoff. "What is your question?" Even cool, calm, and collected Geoff looked nervous. In a soft voice, he told their story about the relationship with their friend, about how he had died of a heart attack on the golf course five years ago. He told her about the yellow sticky notes with their friend's signature. Then he told in great detail about what happened on the golf course yesterday. Peter, Art and Icon listened and nodded vigorously in agreement as Geoff recounted the tale.

Once Geoff was finished, Majilla ask that everyone close their eyes and hold hands, in order to focus on their friend. As they sat thus, very faint eerie music could be heard from a distant room. After a few minutes, she announced in a soft, voice that she was getting a message from their deceased friend.

I sat there taking this all in from the back of the room and knew it was a bunch of bullshit. There was no way she knew I was in the room and she certainly wasn't communicating with me. What a scam! If the guys were gullible enough to believe her, then they deserved to lose their twenty-five bucks. Never the less, I was also here for a little fun, so I didn't want my friends to go away disappointed.

As planned, they had not revealed Jason's name to her and she had not asked.

"What is his message?" Geoff asked, skeptically

"He seems to be saying that he misses you and wishes he could golf with you again."

Well, that was a logical answer. She had been told that I played golf with them for years. So she was correct about that.

"Does he say anything else?" Geoff prodded.

Majilla interrupted, "Be silent! I am listening to him." Majilla had her eyes closed, which now seemed to be her mode when appearing to be in communication with the dead. She silently moved her lips as if she were talking with someone.

"He says that he enjoyed playing golf with you yesterday."

Well it appeared that Majilla, at least was a good listener. What she has said so far, was all a matter of deduction. She knew enough about yesterday and the card signatures that she could get away saying I play golf with them. I was thoroughly enjoying this charade.

Now Geoff started to ask her questions that he really did not expect her to be able to answer.

"Does he say who he is? What is his name?" Geoff nudged

I knew there was no way she could answer this one, but I was sure she would continue the pretense.

Again, she closed her eyes and we heard her humming almost inaudibly. I figured she was trying to figure how she could get herself out of this and still collect $25 bucks. She opened her eyes half way and touched a hand mirror on her table. It appeared to be covered by a chalky film. She picked it up and stared into it, as if to see a face. This reminded me of the scene from Snow White with the evil queen: 'Mirror, mirror on the wall...' That's when I decided to really make this fun.

Majilla held the mirror and included trembling hands in her performance. She stared into the mirror as if someone would be revealed. Then, most likely to buy time, her right hand hit the bowl of bones and teeth, spilling its contents. With one hand, she arranged the items in some kind of special order. As all this transpired, my four friends anxiously waited for some kind of revelation.

Then Majilla added a chant to her act. She said she was again in contact with our spiritual friend and that he was trying to tell her something that she could not quite understand.

Now was the time for my intervention. While Majilla sat chanting with her eyes closed, I reached over her shoulder and used my index finger to write 'Jason' on the mirror the same way I had signed the scorecard yesterday and the sticky notes at The Masters.

When Majilla opened her eyes and saw **'*Jason*'** written on the mirror, she let out a shriek!! She knew that **she** had not written the name on the glass. It took her a moment to collect her wits. I wondered if she thought she had finally communicated with the spiritual world, or if she was just going to take advantage of this, whatever it was. Beads of perspiration formed on her forehead. She stuttered as she looked across her table at Geoff.

"Your friend has spoken to me and revealed his name."

None of them had mentioned Jason's name, so this would be the moment of truth. Maintaining her dramatic scene, she turned the mirror around so they could see the name written in the dusty film. Icon, who never talked about his faith, crossed himself and whispered: 'Holy Mary'. Art, Peter and Geoff had similar reactions. But what was really funny to me was that no one had been more shocked than Majilla herself.

Not knowing what to do next, the guys looked from one to the other. They got what they came for. Geoff reached into his pocket and laid forty dollars on the table. They couldn't wait to get out of that trailer.

Now, as much fun as I had, I almost felt remorse for the trick I had just played on my friends. They had gone to see the psychic on a whim. It had transpired almost as a dare and I had just added to their shroud of unanswered questions.

It had been a hot, muggy morning when they had arrived at Majilla's, so when they left, nearly an hour later, it came as no surprise that a thunderstorm had moved into the mountains. As they hurriedly piled into Art's car, a bolt of lightning struck a nearby pine tree and sent shivers through all of them, only adding to this mystical experience. They could not get down that dirt road fast enough. Not knowing what to make of all this, the four remained quiet.

Finally Peter broke the silence, "I really need a cold beer! How about we go up to Romaine's?"

"I'll vote for that!" Art was ready for something more normal and a beer run up to Romaine's little shack was just what his nerves needed.

Back when we hung around a lot, I had never thought that any of them were particularly religious. But today, as they headed up towards the Blue Ridge foothills, it seemed that this experience might just have convinced them that there could be an afterlife.

Ronnie finally broke his silence. "I don't know about you guys, but for a few minutes while I was sitting there across the table from that gypsy lady, I actually felt Jason in the room with us. I know it was probably just the setting, but damn if I didn't feel his presence."

"I have never heard of anyone actually seeing or talking with a ghost," Geoff added, "but seeing Jason's name written first on the sticky notes, then on our scorecard and now on the damn mirror, is beyond my understanding. It is just weird and I don't much like this feeling!"

It didn't take long before they rounded the curve in front of 'Bob's Place'. This ol' ramshackle bar proudly flew both the American flag and a Confederate flag. According to hearsay, it was the oldest bar in the upstate of South Carolina. Chickens ran free on the grounds and in the bar as well. The restrooms consisted of two outhouses. One sign read 'sitters' and the other read 'shakers'.

The boys entered the windowless bar and nodded to several of the regulars, sporting their biking leathers. Because of the winding mountain roads, this was a favorite for Harley Hogs.

The thunder storm had quickly come and gone, as they typically did in the mountains during summer months. The dusty room was lit solely from rays of sunshine coming through the door. Romaine, the proprietor, was at least 90. You could always find her in a shaded chair just outside the doorway. She only sold four kinds of canned beer. The price was $2. There were no peanuts, chips or other snacks. That was fine with my four friends, as all they wanted right now was beer!

I wandered the familiar room and spotted an old photo of me and one of my best friends, Mike Royster, secured to the wall with a safety pin. I didn't remember ever seeing it before, so figured someone must have put it up after my death. Guess I was more of a regular up here than I'd like to admit!

After putting a $20 bill in Romaine's cash register and making his own change for 5 beers, Geoff and the other three went outside to visit with others who had ventured to this mountain top bar. They sat quietly and sipped their beer for a few minutes. Then Peter noticed the extra beer on the table. "You get me two beers, Geoff?"

In a low voice, so others could not catch their conversation, Geoff retorted, "No Peter! I been thinkin' about what Ronnie said. Although I don't want to believe it, how else could we explain all these strange happenings? I'm beginning to believe that Jason's spirit has visited us several times now and could be with us this minute." With a little mischief on his face, he added, "So, I got him a beer, too." They all had a laugh and raised their cans to cheer Jason. "I'm convinced" Art said: "that Jason was messing with us yesterday. You guys all know that we don't play that well...ever! He had to be there helping us make those birdies on number one...and the eagle as well. I mean the odds of all four of us all making a birdie on the same hole would be a million to one."

After several more beers, they decided it was time to head home. When they stood up, Peter noticed that 'Jason's' beer can was still there, "You're not going to leave that beer are you Geoff?"

"I told you it was for Jason." Geoff replied adamantly.

"Ya, but since he can't really drink it, I'll just finish it off for him," offered Peter. But when he picked up the can, it was empty.

"Hey, who drank this? I didn't see anyone touch this can. Peter retorted.

They all looked at each other to see whose face cracked first. One of the four of them had to have consumed that beer! Right?

## Last Round of Golf

Ronnie whispered, "Hold on a minute. With all that has happened, starting with The Masters a few years ago, then yesterday on the golf course and just now with the empty beer can, I think we have to admit that Jason has been with us. Agreed?"

Peter responded: "I think I do. And don't forget the spookiest part...his name on the mirror."

Both Art and Geoff shivered, as if to remove any remnants of the fortune telling visit.

"Ok." Icon continued, "Let's all stand in a circle and put our arms around each other's shoulders, but leave a space for one more."

"Why?" questioned the other three in unison.

"What are we going to do, pretend that Jason is with us and the empty space is for him?" asked Art.

"Well," continued Ron, "We are playing golf together again tomorrow, right? I just thought it would be nice to invite Jason to play with us again."

"You're crazy Ronnie!" Peter blurted.

"Whyyy not?" Ronnie sometimes stretched out the words when he was making a point.

"Hurry up before the bikers up there see us." Art blurted.

"Alright here we go," Icon continued. "Jason, if you are among us today, we invite you to play golf with us tomorrow. Our tee time is 11:06. Be there if you don't have anything else to do."

This drew chuckles from the other three and they hoped no one would ever find out about this childish ritual.

I would indeed join them for a final round of golf tomorrow before I had to return to my tomb.

\*\*\*\*

It was a beautiful Sunday morning and I was there promptly at 11:06am. The guys were already in their carts and headed for the first tee. Now that my friends believed that I was with them, I planned another fun day on the golf course.

Geoff was the last to tee up. When he bent to place his ball on the tee, the rest did not notice that he had also placed a second ball on a tee a couple of feet away.

Before Geoff hit his drive, Art noticed the other ball. "No confidence today, Skippy? Is this for your mulligan?" he asked.

"No." Geoff said emphatically, "I set that one up for Jason."

"Now that's the spirit Skippy, very nice of you." chimed in Ronnie.

When Geoff struck his ball, it was a good one. The drive did not reach the distance that he and I hit together on Friday, but it was very respectable.

While they were congratulating Geoff on his drive, I went over and picked my ball up and at the speed of light took the ball and placed it on the green, 330 yards from the gold tee.

After Geoff made sure he saw where his drive landed, he turned to pick up Jason's ball. But, it wasn't there. "Where did Jason's ball go?" They looked at each other and shook their heads in bewilderment. The tee was still stuck in the ground, so Geoff just picked it up and dropped it in his pocket.

"What kind of ball was it?" Peter asked.

"It was one of those new OnCore balls they are pushing up in the pro-shop. Cost me almost four bucks. I hate to lose it!"

Before any of them took their second shot, Art noticed my ball. "Hey, looks like somebody left a ball on the green."

Their second shots weren't bad. One was just short of the green and three found the green.

Once they were all on the green, Ronnie walked over to pick up the ball Art had noticed.

"Hey, this is one of those OnCore balls, Geoff."

"Holy Shit!!" Ron stammered.

"No way!" Art blurted out

Well, they had invited me to play, so play I would!

Peter asked, "Do you think this is a coincidence or do you think Jason is really here with us this morning?"

Ron handed it over to Geoff and he made an ink mark on it and put it back in his pocket.

The guys were still a little wary with what happened on Hole #1, but I thought they were beginning to accept me. Hole #4 was a 137 yard par 3. Most of the time they could pitch it onto the green.

What I did next blew their minds. Very carefully, I reached into Geoff's pocket and got out the extra ball he was carrying and headed up to the green before they hit.

Ronnie chipped his ball within range of a par and both Peter and Art hit shots that would make easy birdies. They marked their balls and removed them. Geoff's shot also made it to the green, but was not quite as close as Ronnie's. It missed going in by about an inch and rolled beyond the hole. He marked his ball allowing Icon to make an easy par.

"All right!!" Ronnie roared as his ball dropped into the hole. When he reached down to retrieve his ball, he found two balls in the hole

"Weird, there are two balls in this hole." He removed both balls.

"You're not going to believe this," Ronnie said. "On my mother's grave, it is the same OnCore ball you marked a few minutes ago, Geoff."

By reflex, Geoff felt for the ball in his pocket. No ball!

"We all know what's happening," Art added. "Yesterday we did that little circle up at Romaine's and invited Jason to play with us. Well, I think we have ourselves a ghost as a 5th player. He thinks he's funny making a hole-in-one!"

Peter was the excitable one. "This all started off as a joke and now it seems that the joke is on us. I think maybe we need to just quit today and head for the club house. I really need a few beers to calm my nerves."

"Oh, come onnnn." said Ronnie: "Now that we understand he is playing with us today, let's just continue and see what other surprises he has in his bag. I mean, what harm can it do?"

Art, Geoff and Ronnie admitted that Jason had truly made an appearance. But not Peter! He was frightened and didn't want any part of this ghost stuff.

They walked towards the carts and headed for the next hole.

Peter popped another beer and counted how many he had left before getting to the Turn House Grill. He mumbled to Art, "This has to the stupidest thing I've ever done. Aren't ghosts only supposed to come out at night? Here we are in the middle of the day in 84° weather, playing golf with a ghost. Really? Are you kidding me!!?"

"I though you and Jason were good friends." Art said.

"Yea, but he was alive back then."

"OK." Art continued, "I admit that what we are doing is beyond real. But it is what it is. I really thought about what happened at The Masters where we got those sticky notes from Jason. That was wild and we could never figure it out. But after Friday's round, where we all made unbelievable scores, I have to admit, I do believe Jason is here with us. My guess is that he misses us. Let's enjoy his presence while we can. I just hope that when I die, I can come back and play golf with you guys, too." Art's comments had a settling effect on Peter. But, he still needed another beer to maintain his composure.

Hole #5 was 424 yards from the senior gold tees. This time they all accommodated Jason. So Ron teed up a second ball for Jason in case he wanted to hit it. Of course none of them actually expected to see the ball hit. But just for fun Icon had teed it up anyway. Between their drives, again, the extra ball disappeared. When they drove their carts down the fairway, they spotted that marked OnCore ball in perfect position to go over the pond for the green in two. Before they left the fairway, heading toward the green Peter noticed the OnCore ball was no longer there. As they had now anticipated, the ball being used by Jason was on the green about 12 feet above the hole. Once everyone was on the green one of them always had an eye on the OnCore ball. So with all eyes watching, I gave my ball a little nudge with my finger and it rolled towards the hole, stopping within inches. It was always considered a 'gimie' when you got this close to the hole, but under the circumstances, decided I'd better tap it in.

Without seeing a putter, the guys stared in total silence at my ball rolling into the hole. No one said a word. They just quietly moved on to the next hole. Belatedly, Art decided he'd better keep track of Jason's score.

I think they enjoyed that round of golf. Eventually they began to relax...even Peter. They started reminiscing about our times together and finally started talking directly *to* me. Of course I could not talk back. They acted as if I could hear them and when I made some good shots they bragged on me. On the 18th, Geoff talked to thin air.

"Jason, we have had two rounds of golf this weekend like no other. I believe you are here with us because we were all such good friends. We have missed you and once we got used to having you with us in this new way, we've cherished this time. If you ever want to come back, we're here almost here every Friday. We are headed to the Turn House for our usual beers. I hope you decide to join us."

It was late Sunday afternoon and I would need to be heading back to my resting place in Greenville. I knew that after I met with the Tomb Society on Thursday night, I'd probably go back to my casket again...for a long time.

But before I departed, I joined my friends for one last beer.

There was an empty table on the patio with five chairs. So the guys decided to sit out there. Peter ordered a pitcher of beer and five cups. He poured one for each of us. My beer sat in front of the empty chair. When they were not watching, I grabbed that glass and sucked it down in the bat of an eye. It was time to head out, and when they noticed my empty glass, they knew that I was gone.

# **Epilog**

I was met at the mausoleum gates by Wally, who welcomed me back with a warm smile. I spent some time telling Wally about my adventure, and then realized I was mentally exhausted. Time for a nap...until Thursday night.

Thursday night's cocktail party had the usual suspects. I spotted Dan, Jimmy and Vince chatting together. They were anxious to hear about my exploits. Since neither of them was brave enough to venture out, they chose to live vicariously through my misadventures.

Toward the end of the night, I went in search of Wally. After that few days, I wanted to write a letter to my buddies at Lake Keowee. But, I had no way to do this. When I asked him if it was possible, he suggested that I go to the mortuary office on the corner of the property. He felt sure I could find what I needed. If I put the letter in an envelope with a stamp, and the proper address, he was sure one of the staff would just drop it in the mail on Monday.

Around 3:00am I followed Wally's suggestions. It was pretty easy to find the secretary's office and after a short search, I found the mortuary's stationary. I sat down in the chair and began to write. There were no stamps so I searched for the mail room. I found a small room with a copy machine and a basket marked 'outgoing mail', and left the letter among others in that basket.

*Dear Geoff,*

*Although I address this letter to you, it is intended for Art, Peter and Mr. Icon, as well.*

*We were close friends for a number of years. We played a lot of golf and did a healthy amount of partying. I will remember those days for eternity. It was you guys who tried to save me and when all failed, you honored me by helping my daughter arrange for my funeral. It was because of y'all she got through that tough time.*

*I know I've given you a few scares over the last couple of years. And, I don't blame you for questioning that I could be with you after death. When the doctors were unable to save me and my heart stopped, I had what can only be called an 'out of body' experience. Sometimes you'll hear about people who claim they had this phenomenon, and of course, live to tell their story. In my case, I did not come back, but somehow I still exist in a spiritual form. You can neither see me nor can we talk with each other.*

*I really enjoyed my visits with you both at The Masters and last weekend at Keowee Key. I cracked up when the gypsy in Salem saw my* name on the mirror. It was priceless! By now you know that it was I who helped you win your Friday game last week. No harm was done and just between us boys, it was a hoot to rout the usual winners. Sorry about the big bar tab!

If you are ever in Greenville, and have a little time, use your mausoleum key and come rap on my crypt. Who knows, I may wake up and let you know I am still around.

You remember that vow they use in weddings? "Until death do us part." Don't believe it. Some of us never truly go away!

Jason McNeill

**The End...maybe**

Made in the USA
Columbia, SC
13 November 2018